PUNISHING MISS PRIMROSE PARTS I - V

A STORY IN THE RED CHRYSANTHEMUM SERIES

BY: EM BROWN

Table of Contents

GOT HEAT?

"This one made me go WOW! I read it in a few hours which technically I probably should have gotten more sleep, but for me it was that good that I deprived myself of sleep to finish this most awesome story!"

- Goodreads reader review of MASTERING THE MARCHIONESS

"HOT AND FUN TO READ!!!!!!!!"

- Reader review of ALL WRAPPED UP FOR CHRISTMAS

"…sex was intense…thrilling…."

- Goodreads reader review of CONQUERING THE COUNTESS

"I loved this book. Clever dialogue that kept m[e] laughing, delightful characters and a wonderful story. I am not generally one who likes historical fiction but this book carried me along from page one."

- Goodreads reader review of CONQUERING THE COUNTESS

Other Works By Em Brown

Cavern of Pleasure Series
Mastering the Marchioness
Conquering the Countess
Binding the Baroness

Red Chrysanthemum Series
Master vs. Mistress
Punishing Miss Primrose, Parts I - V
Punishing Miss Primrose, Parts VI - X

Other Novels
All Wrapped Up for Christmas
Force My Hand
A Soldier's Seduction
Submitting Again (coming soon)

Other Novellas/Short Stories
Submitting to the Rake
Submitting to Lord Rockwell

Anthologies
Hot Dads: the DILF Anthology
Threesomes
Once Upon a Threesome

For free e-book giveaways and advanced readings, sign up for the
Erotic Historicals
quarterly newsletter at www.EroticHistoricals.com

PUNISHING MISS PRIMROSE
PARTS I-V

Part I

Punishing Miss Primrose

Punishing Miss Primrose, Part I

FROM HIS CHAIR in the far corner of Madame Devereux's dim and tawdry parlor, Spencer Edelton, the third Marquess of Carey, observed the unhappy flutter of Miss Primrose's eyelashes as she stood before Madame Devereux. When first he had set eyes upon Miss Primrose, he had been surprised to find she possessed none of the classic beauty he would have expected of a woman rumored to have had as many conquests as she. No rounded cheeks, delicate lips, or slender nose adorned her countenance. Despite her Scottish surname, her darker complexion and ebony hair suggested a mixed heritage—Moor, perhaps. He frowned to think that both his brother, Nicholas, and his cousin, William, had been bested by such a strumpet.

"I am most sincere when I say I require a respite," Miss Primrose said, her voice coming from a deeper part of the throat than most women. "My last spell as a mistress proved rather wearisome."

Mistress. Spencer narrowed his eyes. His grasp tightened about the gloves he held as he recalled the contents of a letter he had discovered in Nicholas' bedchamber. *Mistress Primrose*, it had begun.

To calm himself, he turned his attention to the fake Persian carpet, the heavy damask curtains draped about the lone window, the tarnished candelabras tacked upon walls covered in worn dull silk, and a longcase clock whse arms did not move. The surroundings reminded him of how remiss he had been in looking after his younger brother. He ought to have placed a tighter rein upon poor Nicholas and limited the latter's friendship with William, a dubious influence.

"This *gentleman* you speak of will be far happier with another choice," Miss Primrose added when she had received no response from her employer. She had not noticed or chose to ignore his presence in the room.

My dear Beatrice," the older proprietress attempted, "with your skills—"

"Libby is far prettier."

Madame Devereux relented. "The gentleman requested you by name. Apparently he has heard tell of your reputation."

"Molly is adept with the dominant role."

"Perhaps he is partial to a more exotic experience. Our patrons are not exactly men of ordinary tastes, are they? Moreover, the price is more than right."

"The bugger has money then," Miss Primrose said, unimpressed.

"Money and peerage, I suspect."

The information only made Miss Primrose frown more.

"You would be well compensated for your time," Madame Devereux coaxed.

"Have you the money?"

"He advanced us fifty quid. And another fifty will be paid upon satisfaction."

The amount seemed to give Miss Primrose pause. Nonetheless, she replied firmly, "No. I have done with fancy bastards."

Spencer shifted in his seat at this unexpected response. How could money fail to persuade? Was it not the sole objective of whoring? Granted, she had already exacted a grand sum from Nicholas and William, neither of whom were particularly frugal or discrete with their funds. But she could have had more. She could have aspired to a courtesan and leave the pitiful brothel that Madame Devereux kept, though the patroness insisted that the Inn of the Red Chrysanthemum was not a whorehouse but a club where members indulged their penchant for taboo pleasures.

When Spencer had confronted his brother, Nicholas had admitted to patronizing the Red Chrysanthemum, and claimed he was in love with Miss Primrose and had hoped to tempt her away from the place with all that a woman of her situation could ever hope for and more: a townhome, servants, and an allowance for gowns and baubles. Spencer had never seen the poor boy so desperate, yet *she* had cast off *him*, refusing to ever see him or William again. Perhaps Miss Primrose was not in possession of all her senses. Or perhaps she played a game, as many women were wont to do, withholding her favors to encourage an even greater offer, though Nicholas had already promised her more than his means. At least Nicholas had enough sense not to propose the ultimate prize: marriage.

But Spencer, unsure that his brother would not eventually succumb to such a misstep, had his uncle take the two young men to Belgium, hoping time and distance would remove the influence of Miss Primrose. William—easily pleased with wine, women, cards, and horseflesh—was more likely to recover. Nicholas, however, possessed a more delicate constitution. Spencer had never seen a man look as despondent, beaten, and woeful. His younger brother was a mere shell of a man. Spencer did not doubt that, given the chance and despite her treatment of him, Nicholas would crawl, like a pathetic little puppy, back to Miss Primrose.

Something had to be done about her. The quality of her speech suggested she had not been raised in the lower classes, but at best, she was of the bourgeoisie. For her to trifle with men of superior position showed tremendous insolence, a flagrant audacity that was not to be tolerated. Miss Beatrice Primrose required a set-down. She needed to be taught a lesson.

"Beatrice, please," Madame Devereux implored, lowering her voice. "How often does fifty quid—in advance, mind you—come our way?"

"I did more than fifty quid for you by way of Nicholas Edelton and that craven cousin of his."

A muscle tensed along Spencer's jaw. Nicholas had admitted that, once his own allowance had been exhausted, he had taken to borrowing from friends to sustain Miss Primrose. Spencer briefly wondered that the woman, with all that she had swindled from Nicholas and William, had not procured herself a better frock than the one she currently wore. The fabric was wearing thin and the hem repaired in several places.

"For which I am eternally grateful," Madame Devereux said. "If you accept this occasion, I will have no need to call upon you for a long, long time. You may enjoy your well-earned reprieve, free of concerns. Allow yourself an indulgence. Perhaps take yourself and James to Bath."

James. She had a lover. Perhaps this fellow was why Miss Primrose had dismissed Nicholas, Spencer thought.

"But the man wants a whole sennight?" Miss Primrose replied with a shake of the head. "What sort of man asks for a bloody sennight?"

"A lonely one."

"A lecher."

Madame Devereux arched her brows. "Do we service any other kind of patron?"

Miss Primrose curled her lips. "And I am to travel to his abode? Why does he not come here?"

"He does not reside in town. It would be an inconvenience."

"My equipment is here."

"He has offered to transport most of it and make a carriage available to you."

Miss Primrose contemplated in silence, then crossed her arms. "A hundred quid you say?"

"He is flush in the purse. If he is pleased, perhaps an additional perquisite will come our way."

"A hundred quid be a lot to pay for any wench. He must be homely as the devil. Is he an albino like the one that made Jane retch?"

"On the contrary, he is by far the most handsome man to walk through our doors. You're right lucky, Beatrice. Any number of girls would stumble over themselves to lift her skirts for him—gratis."

"Then what's wrong with the fellow? If he is as endowed in body and funds as you claim, he would have no need to come to us."

"You forget he has a specific interest in *you*."

"What of me interests him?"

Madame Devereux sighed and put a hand to her temple. Sensing the proprietress was on the verge of relenting, Spencer rose from his chair and advanced till he had the attention of both women. He stood behind Madame Devereux and allowed Miss Primrose a moment to assess what she saw. Her gaze took in his rugged build, which he knew to be well accentuated by his talented tailors. Blessed in countenance and form, he expected Miss Primrose to be pleased with what she saw, and her frown did dissipate, but it was fleeting.

"Do you require assistance, sir?" she asked.

"I am the patron being discussed," he supplied, his manners compelling him to make her a bow though she deserved none of it.

She remained collected. "And you are?"

"My name would serve you no purpose."

"But you have heard of mine?"

"Nicholas Edelton spoke of you with great…admiration."

He forced the word, trying his best to contain his anger. He risked revealing his relation by speaking the name of his brother, but the two bore little resemblance, almost as if they had been born of different parents.

"You are a friend of his?"

"No."

The answer lessened her frown.

"Nonetheless, the vehemence with which he spoke caught my attention. He seemed quite taken by you."

"And you pay Nicholas Edelton such regard that you would lay down fifty quid for me?"

Spencer straightened. It was clear she did not hold Nicholas in much esteem. He did not fault her for lacking much admiration for Nicholas, who struggled in the shadow of his older brother, but it made her actions far more callous that she bore no goodwill toward him.

"I once attended an impressive performance of *Antony and Cleopatra,*" he said. "The Queen of Egypt is a remarkable vision. It has been a desire of mine to seek her likeness."

Madame Devereux looked at Miss Primrose as if to say, "There you have it."

Miss Primrose studied him a while longer as if to make him flinch beneath her gaze. He did not.

"Advance a hundred quid, another hundred upon completion, and perhaps I will consider your proposition."

He suppressed the urge to choke—or ring her neck. The harlot was beyond insolent, though her greed should not have surprised him.

"The original offer is not rich enough that you must double it?"

"If you could part with a hundred, two hundred would be of little difference for a man of your means."

He struggled to maintain his composure at her impudence, then reminded himself that it was a small price to pay for the chance to avenge his brother. He took a deep breath.

"Very well, Miss Primrose. We are agreed."

*****

Beatrice shook her head as she mended the tear in her petticoat with needle and thread. The man had to be mad, though his eyes had gleamed with intelligence and his speech had been articulate and collected. Not even Nicholas Edelton would have been inane enough to offer two hundred quid to bed a strumpet. While wealth allowed men to indulge in the ridiculous, her instinct told her something was not right about the situation. For a man who desired her enough to pay an absurd amount of money, he seemed to have little interest in seducing her. No libidinous smiles, no compliments dripping with lust, no attempts to win her with wine and song.

"Perhaps he is merely awkward with women," Devereux had

suggested when she had shown Beatrice the hundred quid that had been delivered the following day.

"Or he supposes money sufficient to move mountains," Beatrice had thought aloud.

"Does it not? And if you've plenty to spare, why not bandy it about?"

Beatrice was fairly certain she had affronted the man with her demand for twice the initial amount. He was a fool to agree to it, but might she be an equal fool to refuse such a sum? She thought of James and how quickly the boy was growing. It seemed his great-aunt was always writing about how he needed new shoes and new clothes. Soon he would need schooling, too. The expenses would only increase.

"And boys'll eat your day's wages in one meal," Libby, with whom she shared a room at the Inn, told her. "I saw your gent. Wouldn't mind a tumble with that one, I tell you."

Beatrice did not disagree that the man was fine to behold, but she had no intentions of lifting her skirts for him. That was the beauty in being a Mistress and not a submissive. She possessed the libidinous urgings of a healthy woman, to be sure—having reached the age of three and twenty, those desires had only intensified over time—but she had not joined the Red Chrysanthemum to fulfill her prurient interests. Her mentor, a member of the Red Chrysanthemum known as Mistress Scarlet, had taught her that a Mistress must never relinquish control, and, by withholding her own body, she may increase her dominance.

But in the small interaction she had had with this new patron in Madame Devereux's parlor yesterday, Beatrice had not detected any indications that he would truly enjoy playing the role of the subservient. Granted, she had seen men of great standing, from ruthless businessmen to military generals, whimper like a kitten beneath the whip or boot of a proper Mistress. The Red Chrysanthemum had certainly shown her that the bedchamber was capable of coaxing different temperaments and behaviors from the most straightforward of characters.

"Have you once *enjoyed* yourself in your time here?" Libby asked.

"You've forgotten Jonathan."

"Jonathan? You used him to make Nicholas jealous."

"True," Beatrice admitted.

Libby shook her head. "You're an odd one, Bea."

Beatrice said nothing. She had told no one that her only reason for patronizing the Red Chrysanthemum was to exact revenge upon Nicholas Edelton and his cousin William for what they had done to her sister, Charlotte. And with each passing day, the likeness James bore to his father only deepened.

"If I had a chance at your gentleman," Libby said, "I would make a right good time of it. Even if he proved a pitiful lover, if his cock be decent, I should have no problem fucking him at all. I be wet just thinkin' on it."

Watching Libby fan herself, Beatrice allowed herself a chuckle. Perhaps Libby was right. She had accomplished her mission of retribution. While she could have exacted more penance and thrown him deeper in debt by becoming his mistress, she did not think she could tolerate Nicholas much longer. His presence fueled an anger and pain that proved, over time, exhausting. Perhaps she needed to bury the fury and the sorrow. Surely Charlotte would not have wanted her untimely death to extinguish her sister's own chance of happiness.

"A decent lover would suit," Beatrice allowed.

Libby brightened. "Or he might be a superbly skilled lover!

If that be the case, you must let me have a turn with him. What a lucky bit of skirt you are!"

Beatrice recalled the gentleman's tall, wide brow, the wave of his lush light brown hair, and the line of his sensuous lips. Though she was taller than the average woman, he still stood a head taller than she, and she liked the length and strength of his frame. Perhaps she had come across a bit of luck and ought to have a little fun with it and make use of the Red Chrysanthemum's true purpose.

Putting aside her misgivings, Beatrice resolved that she would allow herself to be selfish and indulge her carnal desires with the handsome gentleman. The exchange of money meant she was no different than a common whore, but she had long come to terms with what she did or there should be no support for James. Their aunt could not otherwise afford him, and the thought of James in an orphan asylum was something Beatrice would not entertain.

Pulling out a portmanteau from beneath her bed, Beatrice began to pack.

*****

Several hours from London and with two stops at posting inns between, the carriage pulled up before a two-storied dwelling built of Bath stone. Given how he had parted with a hundred quid with relative ease, Beatrice had expected to find a house like the many palaces of Chelsea and was surprised to find a more modest manor. Nonetheless, she counted twelve windows in its façade and the hedges growing between them had been neatly trimmed.

"Blimey," said Allison, the newer servant girl Madame Devereux had been willing to part with to serve as Beatrice's abigail. Spending a sennight with a stranger was no small matter, and Beatrice could not help the feeling that she could not trust the man entirely.

"You landed a rich one, miss," Allison continued as she stepped from the carriage.

Allison hailed from the country and had been but a fortnight in London. She stood in awe of almost everything she saw.

A footman took their baggage and placed them in their perspective rooms. As it was nearly the time for supper, Allison first assisted Beatrice into her evening dress. Beatrice chose her best gown, a fine muslin with short sleeves and a ribbon at the waist. The women of more polite society would deem the simple white dress ordinary, but it draped well upon her body. As she had put on a little weight since the dress was first sewn, the wide neckline displayed the swell of her breasts more than she would have liked for there was no need to call further attention to the fact that she was here on wanton purposes. She wrapped a colorful Turkish shawl about her at an attempt for more modesty. A bandeau secured her thick hair, and a few short curls framing her face softened the look. A pair of earrings would have finished off her ensemble, but she owned no jewelry.

The gentleman stood waiting for her at the dinner table. He seemed taken aback by her appearance; she supposed she must not have appeared particularly alluring that day he had visited the Inn of the Red Chrysanthemum, but by his current pause, his opinion of her might have improved. Now that she felt more receptive to her sojourn with him, he improved easily in her eyes. He looked quite dapper in his black tailcoat, ivory waistcoat, and layered neckcloth.

"Miss Primrose," he greeted stiffly and pulled her chair for her.

"Mistress Primrose," she corrected.

To her surprise, he frowned and the muscle along his jaw tightened. Without word, he went to sit at his end of the table.

Perhaps he only plays the submissive in the bedchamber, she reasoned to herself. The long table made conversation a little difficult. As he was the host, she expected him to begin the dialogue, which he could have easily done by inquiring after her trip or the condition of the roads, but he was silent as the servants poured the wine and set the first course, a rabbit stew, before them.

"My compliments to your cook," she said after several spoonfuls. She had never tasted such freshness.

He only nodded. They finished the soup in silence. Despite the distance, she could sense his tenseness. Was it the presence of the servants that made him taciturn? Was he, by nature, timid? But he had asserted himself without hesitation at the Red Chrysanthemum. It almost seemed as if he were *displeased,* but Beatrice could hardly guess why, save that perhaps he now harbored second thoughts about their agreement.

"The weather is bit cool for summer," she tried when they were halfway through the second course.

He waited until the servant had finished refilling his wineglass before replying, "There is no need to attempt a *tête-à-tête,* Miss Primrose. You are not being compensated for conversation."

She stiffened at his brusque words but decided not to take offense. In truth, she was not here for his colloquy either.

"Indeed," she agreed. "My services are of a much more *exceptional* nature."

He did not share her mirth and simply resumed his repast.

What an odd fellow, she thought to herself as she tasted the third course, venison with stewed apples. At least the dinner was enjoyable, being one of the finer meals she had ever consumed. The lack of dialogue made for an awkward time, but she granted he had no need to impress or entertain her. His hundred pounds had permitted that. But for a man who was about to have his carnal desires fulfilled, he looked remarkably gloomy.

"You have the benefit of my name, but I know not how to address you," she said at another attempt at civility.

"'Your lordship' will suffice," he replied without looking up.

She raised a brow. "At all times?"

"Yes."

"Including the...when we..."

This time he looked at her. "Yes."

Her mouth dropped. This was not what she would have expected from a man who wanted to submit himself to a Mistress.

"And without fail, Miss Primrose."

She racked her brain to recall what Mistress Scarlet might have said about unorthodox behavior from a submissive. Mistress Scarlet had said that sometimes a submissive might deliberately misbehave in order to merit punishment. A brat, Mistress Scarlet had called them.

Feeling the need to assert her role, Beatrice said, "That does not suit me. If you will not provide a more appropriate name, you may remain nameless."

He stared at her as if he meant to pin her to her chair. "What did you prefer with Mr. Edelton?"

"My pet."

It was a term Mistress Scarlet often used with her partners.

"That, most assuredly, would not suit me," he said, glowering.

It was her turn to frown. It was not his position to set the terms. She decided not to pursue the matter. She required no name for him.

"If you are experiencing reservations or are reconsidering our arrangement," she said after a sorbet with sweetmeats was set before her, "do not worry of offending me, but know that your initial payment is forfeit."

She knew she risked upsetting him—and by the darkening of his eyes, she surmised she had—but she did not want him to entertain the belief that he could expect a return of his money.

"Our arrangement stands, Miss Primrose, but the second half of the payment is contingent upon your satisfactory completion."

"Were you able to convey my, er, implements from the Inn?"

"I have all that is required."

She met his gaze across the table. There was a hardness in his features that unsettled her, but he turned his attention to his dessert before she could examine it further.

"This is a delightful sorbet," she said to lighten the mood. "As good as any found at Gunter's."

His hand tightened about the spoon he held. He set it down and tossed his napkin upon the table but waited patiently for her to finish. She wondered what she had said to vex him.

"You may wait in your chamber until further notice," he said when she had finished her sorbet.

His command took her by surprise, but she obliged and headed back to her room. She could not help but feel disappointed. He had paid a good sum for her favors, yet behaved as if he wanted none of her company. Perhaps she had been too accustomed to the doting attentions of Nicholas. Or perhaps his lordship no longer found her appealing—an unusual circumstance for she had never before failed to garner a look of appreciation from the opposite sex. No doubt it was too much to expect that a man endowed with countenance, wealth, and peerage might also be in possession of charm and wit.

*****

Spencer paced the anteroom of his chambers before heading to the sideboard to pour himself a brandy.

My pet.

He shivered in disgust. Her mention of Gunter's had further incensed him for the tea shop was a favorite of Nicholas'. It was there that a friend had spotted Nicholas with a "mysterious young lady" who was not known in their circles. Spencer had paid no heed until he discovered those disturbing letters, the nature of which were so strange, he hired a former Bow Street Runner to follow Nicholas. The accounts of what the informant provided had appalled him. He wondered that Nicholas could allow a woman to treat him in such fashion.

Nothing in the letters Miss Primrose had written indicated she bore Nicholas any true affection, only contained promises of bawdy carnality and demands for additional funds. It was clear Miss Primrose used Nicholas and William for money and to satisfy her own vulgar cravings to debase her fellow human beings. Spencer could not require her to return the money Nicholas had freely given to her, and as he could not have her imprisoned without exposing his brother and cousin, he decided he would give her a taste of her own medicine.

For a woman who had lured a considerable sum of money, however, she showed no evidence of it. Her gown tonight was passable—he had to admit she looked quite fetching in it—but she could have afforded better. He knew no woman who would not take the chance to spend a part of her allowance on new gowns, bonnets, baubles and the like. Why would a woman like that horde her funds?

It was none of his affair, he reminded himself as he downed the brandy. As he recalled the vision she presented upon entering the dining room, he could see how a man might succumb to her beauty. She had kept the shawl about her the whole of the evening, but it had slipped often from her shoulder, exposing the bareness of her upper chest. Given what he intended with her, he knew not if it was fortuitous or inauspicious that he should deem her attractive.

He poured himself another glass. He had not quite thought out the whole of his plans, but he knew he wanted her to appreciate the pain and humiliation she had put Nicholas through. He might demand that she write a letter of apology to Nicholas. Spencer hoped in some way to restore what she had taken from Nicholas. And punish her for what she had done. He had had a mind to make her his prisoner for the sennight for surely she belonged in Bridewell. She deserved to be locked in her room and served nothing but bread and water.

But he could not do it—yet. His brother and cousin were not blameless in the matter. If she had confined herself to milking them for money, he would not have been pleased, but he might have restrained himself to a stern talk with her and a warning to stay away from his family at her peril. But she had not. Rather, she had seen fit to demean Nicholas, to use his lust against him and strip him of his manhood. The descriptions from the informant of the treatment Nicholas had received at her hands had made Spencer tremble with rage. No one treated a member of the Edelton family with such callous disregard.

No one.

*****

Having sat nearly an hour in her chamber with nothing to entertain herself but the mirror, Beatrice realized a Mistress would not sit idly waiting for word. A Mistress decided what was to come next. The unfamiliar circumstances—instead of the comfort of the Inn of the Red Chrysanthemum, she was a guest at *his* house—had momentarily jarred her from her character. Perhaps *his lordship* did not fully understand the roles they were to assume. Wrapping her shawl about her, Beatrice picked up a lamp and decided to explore the premises.

Expecting to find mostly bedchambers on the upper floor, she headed downstairs. The décor matched the master of the house: stately and not ostentatious. She passed through the hallway and a room she suspected to be the drawing room. Above the fireplace hung a painting of an older man and woman. A husband and wife, Beatrice suspected. Upon closer inspection, the man in the painting could very well have been the father of *his lordship*. Both men had a serious air to them. The woman, too, looked familiar, but for reasons Beatrice could not place.

After spending a few moments admiring the furniture, the silk wallpaper, and paintings of a country estate, she proceeded to the next room. It was a library. The low fire in the hearth suggested the room had been occupied earlier in the evening. The curtains had been drawn over the windows and the candelabras no longer lit. With sofas, winged armchairs, and alcoves brimming with pillows, the room offered many inviting places to sit and read. Beatrice approached a wall of books and looked at the various titles. She had not had the luxury of reading in some time. She was unacquainted with most of the works until she came to a novel by Daniel Defoe.

She removed the book from its perch. *The Fortunes and Misfortunes of the Famous Moll Flanders, &c.*

"I thought I told you to wait in your chambers."

The voice at the entrance startled her, and she dropped the

book. Turning, she held up her lamp. His lordship stood with his hands at his hips. He had removed his coat, and his hair was slightly disheveled, as if he had run his hands through it several times. There was a gloss to his eyes that she had not noticed during dinner.

"A Mistress does not receive commands. She gives them," she informed him as if he were her student. She set the lamp on a table nearby.

The corner of his mouth twitched, as if he were about to smirk.

"And you take great pleasure in commanding others," he said as he advanced toward her.

Did he mean to accuse her? she wondered.

He stopped and picked up her book, noting its title. "How fitting."

She narrowed her eyes. "Your pardon?"

"Have you read it?"

"Some years ago."

"And do you find a kindred spirit in the heroine, a whore, thief, and felon?"

The antagonistic edge in his tone made her defensive. She snatched the book from him, though it was his property.

"Through Moll Flanders, the author has painted the plight of women with great sympathy. One cannot help but admire the determination and resourcefulness of Mrs. Flanders."

"A woman of loose virtue, dishonest, scheming—by her own admission. In the end, she and her husband live in sincere penitence for their wickedness."

"A luxury not afforded to many."

He paused in thought. "You believe her actions were compelled by her circumstances."

"A woman must make her own fortune and seek her own justice. She cannot expect these will be granted to her in any easy form. She may be the most moral and honest and intelligent creature, but these virtues are not always awarded. And if a wrong be done to her, who will defend her? Will it ever be made right?"

Seeing his look of surprise, she realized she must have spoken too vehemently. She glanced away to hide her emotion.

"An unfortunate reality," he said, after a pause, with more compassion than she expected. "But one's circumstances, no matter how dire, do not absolve a man of wrongdoing."

"You would that a beggar submit to starvation rather than steal a loaf of bread?"

"Are your circumstances comparable to that of a beggar?"

She stared at him. Why would he ask such a question? What a strange evening this had become! Though she was partly excited to be engaging in a discussion on the merits of virtue—she could think of no one of late with whom she had had such interesting discourse, and he had listened to her opinions without hastily dismissing them—it was wholly unexpected, leaving her perplexed and a little rattled.

"My circumstances are no affair of yours," she said.

Hoping to place some distance between them so that she could compose her thoughts, she turned away from him, but he reached for the bookshelf beside her, blocking her path with his right arm. He was now closer to her than ever, and she detected the aroma of brandy upon him. Her pulse quickened. She had neglected to devise a strategy for her engagement with this patron, and she sensed the danger of not having done her due diligence, especially as she found herself responding in a most inconvenient fashion to his nearness.

"And if I make it my affair?" he breathed upon her.

Steeling her nerves, she turned to face him, her back pressed against the bookcase. "Surely you did not pay a hundred pounds to hear me tell a tale of woe?"

He was close enough that if he lowered his head, their lips could touch, and for a second, curious if he might prove a good lover, she wished he would kiss her. His right hand came off the bookcase and cupped the side of her face. With his thumb, he tilted her chin up. His fingers came to rest upon the nape of her neck. She became acutely aware of her vulnerability and the difference in their size and strength.

His gaze swept over her physiognomy. "How many men have you ensnared with your loveliness?"

"What does it matter?" she managed to say between uneven breaths. A wealth of sensations began to percolate from low and inside her body, sensations that had lain dormant while she pursued her retribution against Nicholas. Released from their cage, they now threatened to overtake her, and she was not unwilling to give them the reins.

"*You* have my attention at present," she prompted, her voice becoming husky of its own accord.

He shook his head. "You'll not fool me, Miss Primrose."

His hand tightened upon her, and for a moment, she wondered if she ought to be more frightened. The lust in his eyes was something she was accustomed to seeing, but the influence of liquor could make a man unpredictable.

"But I'll take your favors all the same," he finished, stepping into her. His leg grazed hers.

Surrounded by the heat and hardness of his body, she felt a familiar agitation warming her loins. She closed her eyes for a moment and took a calming breath. The sensations had come upon her faster and stronger than she had been prepared for.

When she opened her eyes, she assumed her proper stance as Mistress. "When and if I am ready to grant those favors."

"My money. My rules."

He was leaning further into her, and she felt the need to come up for air. Desire pooled low and hot within her.

"Fair enough, but if I am your Mistress—"

"You," he growled, "are the mistress of nothing. You are mine. To command. To enjoy. To torment."

Torment? She thought she heard the word above the beating of her heart.

"In short, to do as I wish, Miss Primrose."

*****

He could see the wild confusion, a little clouded by lust, in her eyes. His blood was pounding too fiercely for him to have the patience to explain anything to her. There was too much of her in his sight, his nose, his touch. She had intoxicated his every sense. Even if she were not the object of his vengeance, he had to have her at this moment. To prove his point, he shoved his hips at her as his mouth descended over hers. The pressure between his legs grew tenfold as the taste of her, the moistness between her soft and yielding lips, enflamed his desire.

She allowed the assault upon her mouth. Her lips parted—or perhaps he had forced them—for his tongue to plumb the depths behind them. He was vaguely conscious of his crushing force, but the more he tasted of her, the more his appetite grew. More overpowering than the strongest of liquors or the most potent of opiates, the feel of her, the scent of her, had an effect upon him that he could not fight. He pressed his body into hers, feeling her hips, her breasts, her thighs against him. She shifted the angle of her hips, and her tongue met his several times. The encouragement cast off all remaining reservation.

His hand dropped from her neck to her breast. Without relinquishing her mouth, he pushed his hand beneath her décolletage to pry one of the full, smooth orbs from the stiffness of her stays. His fervor must have startled her, for she pushed his hand away and tore herself from him. She stumbled and the book fell to the floor once more. He could see her attempting to establish her breath and put some order to her thoughts. In the light of the lamp, he could see the area about her lips flush from his attentions.

Though flustered, she managed to assert, "I am Mistress Primrose. No other proposition was agreed upon."

His body protested her departure. He almost marveled at the effect she had upon him. Either his desire for revenge had augmented his ardor or she possessed some witchcraft. No wonder Nicholas and William had succumbed to her.

"Does it matter?" he returned, advancing toward her.

"Yes," she replied, but she had hesitated first. She took a step back to maintain the distance between them. "If you discovered me through Nicholas, you would have been aware of that—"

"I was aware," he acknowledged brusquely, the mention of his brother prompting his ire, "but it was inconsequential."

The back of her legs bumped into the ledge of a bay window. "Then I think we need to discuss our arrangement."

"As I said, Miss Primrose, you are mine. For a sennight at least."

He saw her look to the opening to her left, and when she moved in that direction, he lunged and caught her about the waist. She landed against the cushions of the alcove with one leg over a pillow and the other foot still upon the floor. Placing a knee between her legs, he pinned her in her place. The better part of him, a sense of *noblesse oblige* that she had provoked with what she had said earlier, the manner in which she spoke about the injustices facing women, objected to his treatment of her. But he had sensed her arousal. She was not without desires of her own. To confirm his suspicions, he reached beneath the hem of her skirts and pushed them up her leg. She fought him, but he fit both her wrists in one hand. Holding her arms above her by the wrists, he continued his ascent with his free hand. She twisted and bucked against him—unfortunate motions for they only fanned the heat coursing through his veins and amassing in his groin.

"The servants!" she tried.

"Dismissed for the evening."

She groaned. His hand had passed the tops of her stockings to the bare part of her leg. His head swam at the softness of her upper thigh, the proximity to that most private paradise of womanhood. With his leg kneeling between hers, she could not bar him access. Slipping his fingers over the curve of her thigh, he triumphed to find her wet, quite wet, between the legs. He brushed a finger against the small nub of flesh there. She let out a shaky moan, then tried once more to free herself, but with only half the energy.

She succumbed.

*****

What a muddle he had made of her. She could not think properly with him stroking her *there*. His forefinger, coated with the moistness of her betraying desire, slid easily against her, eliciting tremors of pleasure throughout her nether region. But this was not how it was all supposed to happen. She knew only the role of a Mistress at the Red Chrysanthemum. If she had known he intended something else, she might not have acquiesced to his proposal.

But her body cared for nothing but his caresses at present. Helpless as he hovered over her and held her wrists above her head, she could not stop his languid teasing of her clitoris. She wished he would hurry and finish the damned torture. Or not. She could not deny how delightful it felt. He rubbed both his forefinger and middle finger against her, the greater surface area making her moan. The tension inside her mounted. Soon she was writhing, but this time, it was not to escape.

"Ahhh," she gasped when he slid the fingers inside her and his thumb took over working her clitoris.

Her cunnie flexed about the intrusion, but the circling of his thumb was nearly as distracting. She shut her eyes against the intensity of his stare. She knew her desire was written upon her face. Her body had a will of its own, and right now, it wanted to spend more than anything. The valley and peaks of sensation, coaxed masterfully by his fondling, had come to a head. She ground herself into his hand, greedily wanting more of his touch. Her back arched. Every nerve within her now screamed for release. Sensing this, he quickened his ministrations and bore down harder upon her.

She exploded, her body shuddering uncontrollably, her limbs jerking as the most exquisite waves of sensation wracked over her again and again. He softened his caress until the last of the paroxysm had been released. She could feel her blood throbbing in every extremity, her cunnie pulsing. And for several moments, she remained still for fear that any movement might devastate her body further. Only when she felt she could breathe again did she realize how painful his grasp upon her wrists had been. She opened her eyes and saw that he had sat back against the opposite side of the alcove. Lust gleamed in his eyes, and the erection at his crotch was *very* apparent.

She would not mind a repetition of the divine ecstasy she had just recovered from, though the event had not transpired as she would have expected. Undaunted, however, she resolved more than ever to take command of their arrangement. In a moment of weakness and desire, she had allowed him to manhandle her, but Miss Primrose was not to be trifled with for long.

PART II

Punishing Miss Primrose

PUNISHING MISS PRIMROSE, PART II

"RETURN TO YOUR chambers, Miss Primrose," Spencer advised after a haggard breath, his hardened cock making speech difficult. He would distance himself farther from her, but his back came upon the corner of the bay window.

She looked up from his bulging crotch in surprise. The fire in the hearth had burnt down to embers, but the whites of her eyes shone brightly even in the dim lighting of the library. No doubt she had expected him to demand the same attention he had shown her moments ago. He had paid her, after all, a loathsome sum. Did he not have a right to treat her like the strumpet that she was?

But he had grander plans in store for Miss Beatrice Primrose, plans that required him to be in command of his faculties—and his lust. At present, he did not trust himself. The vision of her awash in desire, the feel of her body struggling and writhing, the sound of her moaning her pleasure had made the blood pound in his veins like never before. A wholly unexpected event. And a wicked part of him urged him to relieve the pressure churning in his loins, to use her body as ruthlessly as she had used Nicholas.

"*Now,*" he growled at her.

After a brief hesitation—he sensed she did not appreciate his demanding tone—she complied. When she had left, he sank into the seating area of the alcove. An uncomfortable heat persisted, and the musk of her arousal lingered upon his fingers. His hand itched to bury itself once more in the soft, moist folds between her legs, to push into the depths of her cunnie. His own generosity surprised him. After all that his brother had suffered at her hands, she deserved none of the pleasure provided her. Spencer frowned. Thus far, he had treated her like a guest in his house. She occupied one of the nicer bedchambers. She had dined at his table.

He should have known he was in trouble when she arrived for dinner earlier that evening, looking remarkably fetching in a plain white muslin, devoid of the finery and baubles he had thought would be the ill-gotten gains of her affair with Nicholas. Instead, the simplicity of her ensemble only emphasized her natural assets, among them, rounded hips and an enticing bosom. The brightness of the gown had not detracted from her tanned skin. He suspected she had some mixed heritage that accounted for her color and tight, natural curls, which she had attempted to tame with a bandeau. Though he had claimed to the proprietress of the Inn of the Red Chrysanthemum that he sought the likeness of Cleopatra, he had not thought to find Miss Primrose as attractive as she was.

Cursing himself, he rose to his feet to seek the privacy of his own chambers, located in the opposite wing from where Miss Primrose would sleep. As he reached the top of the stairs, however, he paused. He considered turning down the hall, away from his room and toward hers. If his own desires should overcome him, if he should sink from man to animal and ravish her, it was surely no more than she deserved. But his conscience, his sense of *noblesse oblige*, had been roused by something she had said earlier when he had subtly compared her to Moll Flanders.

"A whore, thief, and felon," he had said.

He could not remember her exact response, but he had seen a flicker of pain in her eyes and heard the vulnerability in her tone. For the first time, he doubted his ability to avenge his brother by making Miss Primrose suffer every lash she had inflicted upon Nicholas. For sure she deserved to be rotting in Bridewell. But it was not against the law to seduce a man and take him for his last shilling when he offered it as freely as Nicholas had. And if Spencer had not compelled their uncle to take Nicholas to Belgium to remove the young man from the grasp of Miss Primrose, Nicholas might have committed the gravest error of all and offered his hand to a common whore.

Spencer shook his head, incredulous. She had turned Nicholas into a despondent shell of a man, had abused him in ways that would make a grown man blush, yet still he pined for her. He remained, despite her mistreatment of him, a sorry little pup at her feet. Having been remiss in looking after his younger brother, Spencer vowed that he would make it right. He would see to it that Miss Primrose would never dare come within an inch of an Edelton again.

He turned in the direction of her bedchamber.

*****

Beatrice looked at the flushed cheeks reflected in the mirror as she sat in the quiet of her chambers. The events of the evening were far from what she had expected. Her hands trembled as she unwrapped the bandeau from her hair. He had sent her back to her room as if she ought to seek shelter from a predator. Though she had not lain with a great many men, she had seen enough of them at Madame Devereux's Inn of the Red Chrysanthemum and was quite familiar with the look of lust in his sex.

"Are you feeling ill, Miss?" asked Allison, a servant girl whom Madame Devereux allowed to serve as Beatrice's abigail for her sojourn with the mysterious gentleman. He had not offered his name, only specifying that she should address him as "your lordship."

Anonymity was honored at the Red Chrysanthemum, an inn where members engaged in illicit and taboo pleasures, and Beatrice would have been at ease if they were back there. Instead, she was spending a sennight at his estate somewhere outside London. Perhaps she had not given careful enough consideration to the situation. Perhaps she had been distracted by his handsome features, his fine manners, and a wish to address her own yearnings, which she had ignored while pursuing her revenge on Nicholas Edelton and his worthless cousin, William.

"Miss? Shall I fetch you a cordial?"

Beatrice collected herself. "I'm quite all right. Thank you."

She smoothed her cheeks as if she could brush away the color, heightened from the orgasm his ministrations had elicited She could not deny it had felt glorious. It had been some time since she had spent with such excitement. In the six months she had been with Nicholas and William, she did not once spend for them. On occasion, she had let them touch her and had nearly retched in revulsion. She could not help but think of how they might have manhandled her sister Charlotte before they raped her.

"What did the servants say about the master of the house?" Beatrice asked as she allowed Allison to unpin her gown.

"His lordship be a bang up-gentleman, eh?" Allison replied. "How lucky you are to have a swell as he wantin' your favors."

Beatrice nearly objected to the word *gentleman*. His courtly bows and politeness had dissipated in the library. She rubbed her wrists, which still ached from his grasp. She grew hot recalling how he had pinioned her arms above her head with one hand while he fondled her most intimate places with the other. She had been unable to hide her arousal from him, but a *gentleman* would not have persisted when she protested. Well, perhaps she had not vocalized her demurral. And perhaps it was of no consequence. He had paid a hundred quid to have her company for the sennight. At that price, he probably felt he owned her.

"'His lordship?'" Beatrice echoed as she stepped out of her petticoats.

"He be a Marquess or an Earl or some such."

That would explain his desire to be addressed with "your lordship," though Beatrice remained perplexed at how stern his tone had been on the subject. At the Red Chrysanthemum, she was known as a *Mistress*, the one in command, to whom the man, or a woman, would submit. "His lordship" thus far had not conducted himself in submissive fashion at all.

"Did they mention him by name?"

Allison shook her head as she began to untie the stays. "Only said he be a bit stern, like his father, but that he be fair and generous during the holidays."

Beatrice rubbed her shoulders. The straps of the stays had dug into them when he had held her arms aloft.

"Peerage, wealth, and countenance," Allison continued with a wistful sigh. "Would I could run me hands through that love'y hair of his. Has he kissed you yet?"

Unaccustomed to such frank discussions, Beatrice colored. She was not a regular member of the Red Chrysanthemum—had used the inn merely to approach Nicholas and William—nor had she often accepted money for her favors. Though she had the impression that *his lordship* thought her a strumpet and little else, she had hoped that the funds from the Edleton cousins would suffice to support her nephew and free her from any lasting whoring until she could find another means of supporting James. A hundred quid—with the potential for another hundred upon satisfactory completion of the sennight—was too rich to decline.

"He did," Beatrice replied as nonchalantly as she could.

"Ah! I envy you, I do, Miss, if you not mind my sayin'. I wouldn't mind his taking liberties with me."

Not wanting to describe in detail what had transpired, Beatrice said, "The library was not a convenient place or time for much more."

"Then more than like he will come tonight for more."

A flutter went through Beatrice at the thought. She had, in part, accepted his proposition to enjoy herself in the manner for which the Red Chrysanthemum existed. As Allison had said, the man had lovely hair—soft golden hair that waved about a wide brow and square jaw. He also had a "love'y" nose, "love'y" eyes and "love'y" lips. He had a nice, lean silhouette to match a set of wide shoulders and a pair of long, strong legs. Her body warmed at the memory of how they had pressed her against the bookcase in the library.

But the thought of him coming into her bedchamber also filled her with apprehension. She did not understand his aloofness, even his grimness. It was almost as if he were obliged against his will to have her here. And he had something, right before he had kissed her, that troubled her. Filled with an agitated heat and distracted by where his body touched hers, she had not caught his every word, but it had seemed he said, *"You are mine. To command. To enjoy. To torment. In short, to do as I wish, Miss Primrose."*

*****

Spencer could hear voices coming from the other side of the doors to her chambers, the higher, shrill voice of the maid and the lower soprano of Miss Primrose. The former did most of the talking while the other answered in near monosyllables. The presence of the maid gave him pause, though he could easily have entered. The maid would know to withdraw at his presence. Surely she knew the purpose for Miss Primrose's stay here. As for his own servants, he had retained a minimal number of the staff and only the few he could trust to be discreet. Since becoming the Marquess of Carey, he had never brought a whiff of scandal to the family name, and if rumors should circulate that he had himself a mistress for a sennight, it would become boring gossip soon enough.

No doubt Miss Primrose was preparing to retire for the evening. He should allow her a good night's rest her first night here. Much lay in store for her. But he could not dispel the disquiet of his body. It wanted her. Much as it would want sustenance after a long spell of hunger. On a whim, he considered seeking relief with the maid. She was not unattractive and had smiled at him when they passed in the halls before dinner. For certain, William would have had no qualms in availing himself of the maid. Nicholas might not either, but Spencer could not exploit a servant in such fashion. And he knew that the maid would only prove a stopgap. Miss Primrose had awakened a dark desire that only she could fulfill.

Rousing himself, Spencer turned and headed back to his own chambers. Once there, he poured himself a brandy—his third of the evening. He cursed himself for a simpleton that he should be so easily tempted by Miss Primrose. He cursed Nicholas and William for their foolishness in seeking out her company. Throwing himself into an armchair, Spencer glanced over to the sideboard. One of the drawers contained the letters Miss Primrose—or Mistress Primrose, as she styled herself—had written to Nicholas, and one that Nicholas had begun to write to her, extolling his love and admiration for her, and begging her to become his mistress in more than name. Nothing in her letters to him indicated she reciprocated his passion, only requests for funds and promises of a bawdy evening at the Red Chrysanthemum.

Also amidst the letters were the reports of a former Bow Street Runner Spencer had hired, upon discovering the letters, to shadow Nicholas. The investigator, a Mr. Fields, had somehow gained access to the Inn. He had declined to meet with Spencer on the details but provided his account in written form of all that he had witnessed between Miss Primrose, Nicholas, and William. After reading the first report from Mr. Fields, Spencer understood the fellow was too fastidious to speak of it in person. Spencer's own blood had run cold and he wondered that he could finish.

The two gentlemen present themselves naked as babes to her, kneeling upon the floor of the room, waiting close to half an hour for her. Their cocks hang in the cool air. She appears wearing naught but her shift and some form of corset that barely covers her nipples. She carries herself in a haughty manner, looking displeased to see them. She holds a riding crop.

If not for his career with the Bow Street Runners, Mr. Fields might prove a talented writer, Spencer thought with a wry smile. He wondered how hard it had been for the man to put pen to paper to describe such a scene. Would he have been aroused by the sight of Miss Primrose?

She commands Mr. Nicholas to stand. When he does, she lifts his cock with her riding crop. It hardens. She smiles and strikes at it with the crop. He howls.

"Thank you, Mistress," he says.

Like a vulture, she circles around him. She applies the crop to his buttocks. He thanks her after each blow. Thin red welts streak his arse. His cock has grown stiff and straight as a maypole. She hits upon the cock once more.

"Thank you, Mistress," he says again.

She asks him if he has been a good pet today?

"Yes," he replies.

She strikes him across the cock and accuses him of fibbing.

He protests it to be the truth.

"If you have not committed a wicked deed, surely you have thought it," she says. "I know you, my pet. You are a wicked little boy. Are you not?"

"Yes, Mistress."

She yanks his head by the hair to her bosom. He kisses it with reverence.

"Confess. What wickedness have you been about today?"

"While playing a hand of brag at the club, I did attempt to look upon the cards my neighbor held. I saw he had a pair of jacks and made my bet accordingly."

"You are a depraved cad."

"Yes, Mistress."

"Only have you confessed your sins shall you be free of punishment. Have you anything else to confess? A sin you neglected to tell me of? A deed from the past?"

"Confess all my wrongs, Mistress?"

"Your greatest crime."

"I have told you the worst."

She reaches for his sac and fondles the pair of orbs within it.
"You lie, my pet, and I detest lies."
She tightens her grip. Mr. Nicholas howls. His screams ring from
the rafters. He collapses in pain.

Having finished his brandy, Spencer lay on his bed and closed
his eyes. If he should require resolve in the following days, he had
but to read one of the reports by Mr. Fields. Then the question
became whether he would be capable of any mercy toward Miss
Primrose.

Though he had not rung for his valet, he allowed sleep to
overcome him. As a young man, before his father had inherited
the peerage of Carey due to a lack of sons by his great-uncle,
Spencer had served on a naval ship and become accustomed to
tending to his own wardrobe. Nicholas, in one of his drunken
moments, had unwittingly challenged a member of The Impress
Service and been pressed into joining the Royal Navy. Doubting
that his younger brother would survive at sea, Spencer had taken
his place, to the great dismay of their father. The senior Edelton
blamed Nicholas for the loss of his first son. Not even upon
Spencer's return did their father forgive Nicholas.

Spencer awoke to an uncomfortable stiffness in his arms, but
he could not move them. He could hear a vibrant crackle from
the fireplace though any flame should have turned to ash by now.
Opening his eyes, he saw that the reason he could not move his
arms was because they were tied to the posts of his bed.

At the foot of his bed stood Miss Primrose.

*****

Holding a candelabra, Beatrice admired his form, his taut

thigh muscles as he attempted to pull at his bindings, for she had tied his arms and ankles to the posts. It had been no easy matter to secure the ropes about his limbs, but fortunately, he had been in a deep slumber, affording her time to coax a fire from the hearth before returning to gaze upon his handsome body.

The look of surprise upon his face turned quickly to anger, which caught her off guard. Nicholas and William had been indignant, but not angry. His lordship was near furious and yanked harder at the ties. For a moment, she worried that he would pull free, but she had learned from the best at the Red Chrysanthemum, a woman named Mistress Scarlet. The bindings held. Beatrice sighed in relief. His lordship was too unpredictable for her, and she would require the bindings in order to impose her desires upon him. She had wanted to take command. How could he excite her as he had in the library but deny her the opportunity to return the courtesy? What sort of game did he play? When he had not come to her bedchambers, she decided it was high time she took matters into hand. It was time she returned the favor from the library.

"Untie me!" he demanded.

"In due time," she replied, then added tauntingly, "*your lordship.*"

He glared at her, but his gaze also took in her appearance. She wore a corset of black satin. It belonged to Madame Devereux, who must have worn it decades ago. Decorative lacing spiraled up the middle. The wide neckline scooped down past her nipples, which could be seen faintly through the shift. The outfit never ceased to cause the cocks to lengthen, and Beatrice allowed her silk banyan to sit upon the edges of her shoulders, that more of her could be seen.

"Untie me," he ordered once more.

She could see the vein at his neck throb, and a shiver of unease went through her. But she could not give ground now or she might not be able to reclaim her dominance later.

Forging ahead, she replied, "I give the orders."

He repeated something he had said earlier. "My money, my rules."

She sighed in exasperation, recalling why she detested rich men. They thought money gave them free rein to do as they wished. They were spoilt, selfish, ruthless creatures.

"Did Nicholas not inform you of how it is to be?" she asked as she set the candelabra upon a table beside his bed. "Perhaps he is not much of a friend."

"Nicholas Edelton is not a friend of mine."

"That speaks in your favor."

He pressed his lips together in grave displeasure.

"This is my house—" he began.

"And it be a stately residence, to be sure."

"The servants are at my beck and call. If I require them…"

"You may shout for them. They may come and untie you."

He was silent. She knew he would not yell for the servants. It would be too much for them to see their master tethered to the bedposts. She knew not what he had told them about her, but she doubted he could explain the situation to their satisfaction.

"You will rue this," he said instead. "I promise you."

She wondered if he had never been bound before? Tying the limbs to the bedposts was tame compared to the other delightful forms of bondage Mistress Scarlet had taught her.

"What was it you had said earlier in the library?" she wondered aloud. "'I'll take your favors all the same,' I believe. As they say, one good turn deserves another."

She slid the robe from her shoulders, lowered herself toward him, and licked the side of his neck. He roared and jerked away from her. He was like a trapped lion, and once again she wondered at the wisdom of what she did. But she would tame this wild beast as she had tamed Nicholas and William. She grasped his chin and forced her to look at him.

"You shall address me as Mistress Primrose at all times. If you behave well and please me, you shall be rewarded. Displease me, and you shall be punished."

He laughed, a hard sardonic laugh. "If you think for one moment I will entertain your vile—"

She slapped him. Hard. The blow surprised him. Now he looked at her in fury. She found it difficult to swallow, but she told herself that if she persisted, she was sure to triumph. William had been difficult at first, but he had eventually taken to his position with enthusiasm.

She returned to her place at the foot of the bed and placed a hand upon his leg. He flinched as if she had the touch of a leper. She trailed her hand up his inner thigh and saw his chest expand, heard the sharp intake of his breath. A thrill went through her as she realized her power. Now she understood why some of the women at the Red Chrysanthemum enjoyed playing this role. She came close to but did not touch his crotch. Instead, she maneuvered her hand along the outer edge of his fall as she climbed onto the bed between his legs. He continued to glare at her.

"There now," she said with a smile as she noticed a slight movement in the area of his cock. "We shall both of us enjoy this, shall we?"

"You will pay for this, Miss Primrose."

"Mistress Primrose," she reminded him.

She settled herself between his legs. A muscle along his jaw rippled. She began leisurely unbuttoning his fine, silk waistcoat.

"Stop this," he hissed.

"His lordship doth protest too much, methinks."

His eyes widened as if insulted that she should quote the Bard of Avon in such a setting.

"Woe that I did not have a gag upon me," she mused.

When she had the last button undone, she flung open his waistcoat. She licked her lips to think what lay beneath. She undid his braces. He struggled against the bonds. He raised his hips but could not topple her from her perch. She curled her fingers into his linen and inched the hem out of his trousers. It skimmed past his torso and up his rib cage, bunching about his neckcloth. She gazed down at the lovely expanse of his chest. Eagerly, her hands spread themselves over the planes of his muscles. His chest rose and expanded with uneven breaths. Lowering herself, she pressed a kiss upon one pectoral.

How delightful that she could take her time with him! With a smile at what lay in store for him, she planted feathery kisses down his midsection to the edge of his trousers. Her bosom brushed against his hardened cock. His breath quickened. She splayed her fingers across his abdomen and contemplated the growing tent at his crotch. A surge of satisfaction went through her. She would show him that it was foolish to resist her, that she held sway over him. If he knew all that she could do to him, he would be much more alarmed than he was.

She tongued his belly button. His body tensed even further. Hovering over him, she licked a nipple of his. His body jerked, though the bindings stymied the motions. She covered the pink nub with her mouth and sucked. He roared, his body bowing off the bed.

"My, how sensitive we are, *your lordship*," she marveled. "I wonder if any wench has ever fondled these darlings before?"

He glared at her. She rolled both rosy protrusions between thumb and forefinger. He groaned between gritted teeth. She returned her attention to the first nipple and flicked her tongue in rapid succession at its hardness. He bucked beneath her, howling. She allowed him a respite, then covered his nipple once more with her mouth. She sucked as if intending to draw milk. In his struggle, his pelvis bumped repeatedly into her. A delightful heat pooled in her groin.

What a rush to have such a strong and virile man, endowed with all that one could desire in life, helpless beneath her! A wicked streak came upon her, and she bit him lightly upon the nipple. He let out a forceful grunt.

"I warn you, Miss Primrose—"

She stared at him with the sternness of a schoolmaster. "If you wish me to stop, you may *beg* for it."

He looked revolted. "Beg? I'll not beg anything of you."

"Suit yourself."

She bit him harder. With a bellow, he jerked at his bindings, and she prayed the bedposts would hold.

"You'll wake the servants," she admonished.

"Damn you."

He looked as if he meant to unleash a torrent of invectives.

She narrowed her eyes. "And I thought you a gentleman."

To punish him, she tortured the nipple without pause, sucking, licking, tugging, gnawing. She applied the same attention to the other nipple. When she was done, perspiration gleamed upon his forehead. His breath came in gasps. A small, triumphant smile tugged at the corner of her lips. His nipples would be sore tomorrow. When he met her gaze, she saw that he had finally realized that she was in control and there was little he could do but submit.

*****

His nipples might as well have been on fire. Spencer had never hated a woman till now. He would have cursed Miss Primrose with words he had never thought to use, but he could not speak while she tormented his nipples. The harlot was beyond belief. If he could free himself, he would fuck her senseless.

For she had extinguished any sense of decency and restraint in him when she dared suggest he beg for relief. Beg. As Nicholas had done. Well, the Marquess of Carey would not give her the satisfaction. What he would give her was retribution. *Noblesse oblige* be damned. As she had suggested, he would be no gentleman. Though he had always conducted himself decorously before the fair sex, Miss Primrose deserved no such courtesy. Despite all that she had done to Nicholas and William, he would not have been surprised to wake in the morning feeling a little abashed at how he had forced his attentions upon her in the library.

But not now.

His cock had never felt so stiff. Every touch upon his nipple had roused his cock further. It strained painfully against his pants. He could not hide it from her. By the smug look upon her face, he surmised she thought it a reflection of his desire for her. He dreaded—and deeply craved—for her to touch his cock.

She seemed to toy with the idea. When she sat back upon her haunches, he was presented with the full surface area of her breasts. They gleamed in the firelight, enflaming him with their beauty. If he could touch them…but his wrists chafed from his struggles against the ropes. He had never felt so helpless, save when the third rate ship of the line he had served upon had come too late to the aid of a merchant vessel. Pirates had ransacked the ship and slashed most of the crew.

Oh God.

She was reaching for his fall. At a slow pace, she unbuttoned the flap and brought it down. His cock sprang free.

"What a lovely Thomas you have," she commented with a sly smile as she studied it. "Such a sturdy length and girth."

His breath caught in his throat. What did she intend to do to him? Would she abuse it as she had done to Nicholas and William?

She slid a finger down the shaft, over the ridges on the under-side. The head of his cock flared at her touch. She pressed her digit to the piss-hole, where his seed had leaked, and drew the moistness down his length. He shivered. God help him.

"You take me for a whore, no doubt," she said. "I do not aspire to pretend that which I am not. But can the same be said of you? Are you a cad dressed in the togs of a gentleman? With the airs of a gentleman?"

The severity of her tone surprised him. He recalled the vehemence with which she had spoken on women having to fend for themselves.

"I think the devil can reside in anyone," she continued. "I think it far more insidious when a man presents himself with civility and gentility but is a blackguard beneath. Perhaps we are all of us at our core, base carnal creatures."

Guilty as charged, he said nothing. Miss Primrose had certainly ignited his own unkind compulsions, testing his restraint and upbringing to the limits. Her philosophical bent intrigued him, and were his cock not pulsing at her hands, he might have engaged in further discourse.

Her gravity dissipated as quickly as it had appeared. She smiled upon his erection.

"Lucky for you, I am no lady."

She lowered her head and engulfed his cock in her mouth. His eyes bulged from their sockets. It had been years since he had lain with a prostitute. Since coming into the marquessate he had confined himself to discreet affairs with opera dancers, and most of them did not swallow cock.

He cursed himself silently. The warmth and wetness of her orifice encasing his shaft felt nothing short of divine. She sucked, and a moan escaped his lips. Her tongue pressed against him, the touch of sublime velvet. Slowly, she began to move her mouth up and down. His toes curled in his shoes. Blood churned hotly in his cods. At times she would flick her tongue over the tip. Or sink till her nose tickled the hairs of his groin, taking in all of him until he could feel the back of her throat.

Hell and damnation.

Pressure boiled in his groin. He would not last long. She wrapped one hand about his cock to keep it steady while she picked up speed. Her other hand reached up and tweaked a nipple. He bucked his pelvis at her. The combination of pain and pleasure was *electric*. He closed his eyes and reveled in the heavenly sensations.

Just as he felt his climax forming, her motions retarded. She stopped. He opened his eyes and saw that she held a small vial. She uncorked it and poured the contents upon his cock. She rubbed it into his flesh. His cock tingled. What manner of villainy was this?

"Be not alarmed," she said. "It is merely a tonic to improve your stamina."

"What the devil—"

She retrieved a long, thin sheath from the pocket of her petticoats. A condom. She pulled it over him and tied the ribbons around his base. Anticipation shot through him. She meant to take him inside of her.

Pulling up her petticoats, she straddled him around the hips. She positioned herself above his cock and sank down an inch.

"Ohhh…." she purred.

He could feel the walls of her cunnie pulsing about the head of his cock. After a moment, she sank down a little farther. She emitted a contented sigh as she adjusted to the feel of him inside her. Her lashes rested against her cheeks, and her bottom lip quivered. She looked beyond beautiful. But she hovered without moving as her cunnie flexed about the top half of his cock. Impatient, he thrust his hips up and speared the whole of his cock into her. Her eyes flew open, but she did not object. Instead, she ground her hot, wet cunnie against him. He had not considered how glorious she would feel. To his surprise, she was much tighter than the whores he had experienced in various ports of call. Though he had wanted to kill her earlier, he could now almost forgive her if he could spend inside of her.

But the condom, or the effect of the strange potion she had applied, dulled his senses enough that his climax loomed like a tall mountain even while she increased the vigor of her motions. His arousal, coming from within, had not diminished, and he attempted to scale that mountain, bucking his hips at her fast and furious. She cried out at the force of it, but rode him equally hard, rubbing that sensitive bud of womanhood against his pelvis.

"Yes, fuck, yes!" she screamed.

And then she spent, tremors racking her body, her wail filling the room. Heat gushed to his cock. He drove himself hard and deep into her, but his climax eluded him. She collapsed onto his chest, shuddering. At first, he allowed her to lay there, though the curls of her hair tickled his nose, to recoup her breath. He felt the dampness of her skin. His cock throbbed inside of her, eager to follow in her wake. He shifted his hips gently, then with greater urgency. She stirred and moaned a little.

When she had fully recovered, she propped herself upon her elbows and looked at him. Having experienced a divine release, her face glowed, and despite her disheveled appearance from her exertions, she looked confoundedly alluring.

"Shall we have another go?" she asked.

By God, yes!

She dismounted from him and inspected his cock. It stood as tall and rigid as before, the condom matted to him. She put a finger to her mouth in contemplation.

Get on with it, he wanted to shout.

Turning, she reached for his ankles and undid the bindings. He groaned as freedom rushed into the stiffness in his limbs. He expected her to undo the bindings around his wrists, but instead, she straddled him once more about the hips, but with her back to him. A novel position. But he cared not a wit how she chose to place herself. He only wanted to be buried in her cunnie. She obliged and settled herself once more upon his cock.

Fuck.

She felt marvelous. The new angle felt marvelous. And with his legs freed, he could propel his hips more easily. He began thrusting into her with the impatience of a schoolboy. She grunted her approval. Her back arched and she rolled her hips in rhythm to him. He felt himself coming to the precipice, to the peak of that mountain, but he could go no further. In contrast, from the sounds she was making, she was heading for another finish. He rammed himself harder into her, deeper into her. Sweat soaked his clothes. What evil concoction had she used upon him? For once, he feared his strength and endurance might give way before completion. She cried out once more, shaking and trembling, then crumpled atop his legs.

He fought back a howl of rage when she disengaged from his cock. Her skin glistened with perspiration. He could see that she was tired and realized he might not spend at all. Was that the intent of this devil-woman? She meant to tease and torment him and deny him as she had done so many times to Nicholas and William. With a furious yank, he managed to wrench one arm free. It was sufficient. He reached for her, scooped her by the waist and threw her upon the bed beside him. She yelped in surprise but did not fight him when he threw up her shift. She lay partially on her stomach, one leg curved atop the other, and he was rewarded with the site of her arse. He might have admired the luscious rump another time, but he was too consumed with need and aggravation. He fit his cock beneath her buttocks and shoved himself into her cunnie. Perhaps too fatigued, she did not resist.

With selfish abandon, he drove himself into her. The bed creaked and swayed to the force of the motions. But again, he was drawn near the brink without the ability to cross. The immense pressure that had been dammed in his body over the past hours was unbearable. He would go mad if he saw no relief. Miss Primrose moaned as he continued to pummel her. The rope about his other arm constricted his motions, but he had no patience to untie it.

"Oh!" she groaned.

Her cunnie began to spasm around his cock. He cursed her. She had used his cock to great effect this evening while his orgasm eluded him. She grew limp, but he persisted for what felt like an eternity. At long last, when the properties of the potion must have worn off, he spent, and it was almost painful. After such a deprivation, he would have expected a grand reward, but the finish was lackluster. He fell back into the bed, gasping for breath, stunned. No sport had come close to necessitating such exertion. Death might have been an easier achievement.

He turned to look at her. She had fallen asleep. Exhausted, he dropped his head back and closed his eyes. He promised himself he would return her favor tenfold. Starting tomorrow.

Part III

Punishing Miss Primrose

PUNISHING MISS PRIMROSE, PART III

BEATRICE PRIMROSE FROWNED. Something was wrong. She had rung three times for Allison, the young servant girl accompanying her on the sennight sojourn with the unnamed gentleman—*his lordship,* as he wished to be addressed—but still the abigail had not appeared.

Eying herself in the mirror, Beatrice attempted to comb her unruly curls into some semblance of order. After her exertions atop *his lordship* last night, she wanted a bath and would require the assistance of the abigail. Sometime in the middle of the night, she had awoken in his bed to find him beside her fast asleep, more exhausted than she. His one wrist was still bound to the bedpost. She untied the rope from him, slid out of the bed, and returned to her own chambers. Not wanting to rouse Allison then, she could not divest herself of her corset and shift, both drenched with his perspiration and her own. She shivered at the memory of how strenuously she had ridden his cock—twice. The tonic she had applied to his cock had ensured he would remain erect for her pleasure, but she wondered if she ought to have introduced it their first night together. He had not been pleased to find himself with a limb tethered to each of the four bedposts.

But then he should not have provoked her with his haughty

demeanor. Such behavior would not have been tolerated by a dominant one at the Inn of the Red Chrysanthemum, where patrons indulged their most wanton and taboo desires. He should not, too, have manhandled her in the library, bringing her to spend, then sending her away as if her presence repulsed him. She had a right to her indignation. In her time as a Mistress at the Red Chrysanthemum, she had never received such treatment. If he had been more agreeable, she would not have had to assert herself last night. Her role as a Mistress was to dominate him, but he had failed to understand this concept. Above all, she wished to prove to herself, and to him, that he desired her. She suspected he viewed her as a simple whore, but whore or not, he was not her superior. And wealthy, entitled *gentlemen* needed to be taught a lesson: that they were no better than their most base and animal instincts.

Conceding to her hair's willfulness for the time being, Beatrice went to the sideboard and poured the pitcher of water into the wash basin. She splashed the water onto her face. Something felt wrong. Though she had set out to accomplish what she intended last night, she wondered if she had roused a sleeping tiger. The look of fury in his eyes had made her hesitate more than once. But her sense of misgiving had existed ever since he had come to the Red Chrysanthemum and offered the proprietress, Madame Devereux, a hundred quid to have the favors of Miss Primrose for a sennight, and another hundred quid upon satisfactory completion. Two hundred quid! Given his handsome features and rugged physique, the man had no need to pay a woman to lie with him, which was why it was such a mystery as to why he would submit such a fine sum to have her.

As she pressed the linen to her face, she heard Allison enter. Without turning about, she said, "I should like a bath drawn before breakfast. I wonder that I have not received an invitation to dine downstairs, but I think the master of the house may require the morning to recover."

"I am faring better than you might think."

She whipped around and saw *his lordship* standing at the threshold. From the sight of him, smartly dressed in buff colored trousers and a dark blue tailcoat, his light brown hair waving over an intelligent brow and molten brown eyes, one would not have expected him to have had a rough night save for the slight shadows beneath his eyes. As Allison had said yesterday, the man was a swell of the first order. Beatrice flushed at the difference in their appearances—she in her undergarments, bedraggled, while he was groomed and dapper.

"Are you in the habit of entering a woman's boudoir unannounced?" she asked with a raised eyebrow.

"I thought you might require some assistance in your toilette."

She almost laughed at such a distinguished gentleman, a member of the peerage according to Madame Devereux, playing the part of a chambermaid. He spoke with calm and none of the rage that she had seen in his face when she had teased and tormented his sensitive nipples last night. But there was still an edge to his tone, as there had often been since she had arrived at his estate.

"That is not a privilege I have granted to you yet."

The man clearly had much to learn.

"What has become of Allison?" she asked. "Has she taken ill?"

He folded his arms. "I have dismissed all the servants earlier this morning. Your abigail is returned to London."

She blinked several times, a little indignant that he would have taken the prerogative of sending her abigail away but mostly stunned that he would not require any of his own servants. What manner of jest was this?

"Dismissed the servants?" she echoed. "Why?"

He pinned her with a solemn stare. "Because, Miss Primrose, I should not wish for them to hear your screams ringing from the rafters."

*****

If not for the seriousness of his intentions, Spencer might have smirked in satisfaction at the shock upon her face. Last night, he had taken a lacing, of sorts, from Miss Primrose, who had tied him to his bed before applying that vicious salve to stall him from spending. He had never had his body used in such a fashion. Were it not for his own intense arousal, he might have felt extremely violated. He had woken sore, stiff, and weary, but he found vigor in his anger. He owed Miss Primrose, not only for what she had done to his brother, but for himself now as well.

Miss Primrose recovered herself. Trollop that she was, she did not seem in the slightest abashed that she stood before him in only her shift and corset, an item from decades ago that flattened the breasts and barely came above the nipples—he was sure they might spring forth at any moment. Despite the draining events last night, his cock stirred. How could he desire this woman? She had abused his brother and his cousin in a manner that went beyond the titillation that the patrons of the Red Chrysanthemum sought. From the accounts provided by Mr. Fields, the Bow Street Runner he had hired, and the grand sums of money she had exacted from Nicholas and William, Spencer was convinced that cruelty and greed were her prime motives.

"Ringing from the rafters?" she echoed with a nervous half-laugh. "Are your skills at lovemaking so exceptional that you can elicit such screams of pleasure?"

He could not help the glint in his eyes. "Your screams, Miss Primrose, will be of a different sort."

Her smile fell, but even then she lost none of her allure. Her dark hair curled in disarray about a smooth countenance. That she had spent a good part of the prior night riding his cock made her disheveled appearance merely wanton rather than unkempt. Everything about her was wanton. Her large brown eyes were fringed with naturally thick and curly lashes. Her lips were much plumper than those of the women of polite society. Her mouth had felt succulent beneath his own. He wanted another taste.

Miss Primrose narrowed her eyes. "What do you mean?"

He adjusted the cuff on the sleeve of his tailcoat. The absence of his valet would be a great inconvenience, but he had roughed it before when the third rate ship of the line he had served on was heavily damaged by Spanish gunboats.

"You shall understand soon enough."

He saw her struggle with indignation and alarm, but she put on a brave front.

"Is such ambiguity intended to titillate?"

He returned a tight smile. "I intend nothing that you are not already familiar with in your time at the Inn of the Red Chrysanthemum."

"And that is to assure me that I have nothing to fear from you?"

He looked at her. If she knew, she might have much to fear. And he almost told her as much.

"I will draw a bath for you," he said instead. He walked over to the hearth to start a fire while trying to quell a desire to toss her onto the bed and fuck her. Hard.

She folded her arms as she watched him. "I've never had a submissive one wish to play the part of the chambermaid, but I am intrigued. Are you playing at Marie Antoinette?"

After stoking a flame to life, he stood and turned to face her. Clearly she expected to reprise her role of *Mistress* Primrose. At the Inn of the Red Chrysanthemum, her sort were considered the "dominant" ones. Nicholas had addressed her as "Mistress Primrose" in his letter begging her to take him back and promising her everything short of marriage. Spencer would be damned if *he* would ever call her that. She did not deserve the slightest courtesy. Though his resolve had wavered yesterday, and though he could not rid his mind of that small moment in the library when pain and sorrow had crept into her voice, she had slain any lingering misgiving when she had restrained him to his own bed and forced herself upon him. She had brought this upon herself.

"Well done, my pet," she said.

He dug his fingernails into his palm. *My pet* was the term she said she had used for Nicholas.

"Are you feigning stupidity or are you truly obtuse as to how it is to be here?"

Her nostrils flared at the insult. Admitting to neither, she remained silent.

"I said yesterday that you are the mistress of nothing. I also specified that you were to address me as 'your lordship,' though 'my lord' would also suit."

"That was not the understood arrangement."

"I know not how *you* understood it, but it was always clear in my mind."

"Then you misled me. You knew my reputation. I have always played the role of the dominant one."

"Then I suggest you learn the role of the submissive one

quickly, for I am not a patient man." He headed back towards the door. "Do you require anything else at the moment, Miss Primrose?"

She stared at him, confounded.

"Then I shall return shortly," he said after her silence. He turned to leave but said over his shoulder, "And when I return, I expect you to address me more properly. I will not tolerate any more of your insubordinate demeanor."

"Insubordinate—!"

"And if you dare call me 'my pet' again, I shall be tempted to flog you within an inch of your life."

He closed the door behind him, leaving her to stew, or fume, over what he had said. Out in the hall, he took a deep breath. He had never threatened a woman before, not even the strumpet he had once caught stealing his coin purse. The quality of *Miss* Primrose's speech suggested she had not been born into poverty. Thus, her whoring must have been a choice on her part. He might have forgiven her the money she had exacted from Nicholas and William, but she had not been content with milking the last mite from them. She had to crush their manhood, their very souls. Having used them, she now discarded them as she might do with one of her condoms. That she had spurned Nicholas's offer to be his mistress—the desperate boy was already borrowing heavily from friends to throw funds her way—gave Spencer only minor pause. When he was through with her, she would never dare lift her eyes to an Edelton again.

*****

Alarm turned into trepidation for Beatrice. She was alone with the man. She had purposefully brought Allison with her in the event that something went amiss. Who would have thought he would turn all the servants away? The man was mad.

She considered bolting from the room, but even if she could escape, where would she go? She knew not where she was. They were a day's trip from London, and they might be miles from anyone. She forced herself to take a deep breath. There was little to be had from panic. True, she should have been more cautious before accepting his proposal. In retrospect, he had provided few details and had been circumspect when she arrived, behaving most oddly for a man seeking to satisfy his lust for a sennight. Foolishly, she had been swayed by his money.

Money was her purpose, she reminded herself. She went to the small writing table and pulled from it a letter that had come from her aunt the day before she left the Red Chrysanthemum. In every letter, Aunt Sophie would express her amazement at how quickly James grew, but in her most recent correspondence, Aunt Sophie wrote,

Forgive the brevity of my last correspondence. James is well and as lively and keen as any boy of his age. But he did suffer a severe fever earlier this month, and I was much afraid for him. I did not wish to write you at the time and worry you if all was to be well in the end. I hope you will not think it extravagant of me that I sent for the doctor several times. The doctor prescribed a great many elixirs to ease discomfort and attempt to lower the fever. We still have ample funds, but a tidy sum was required for the services of the doctor.

Aunt Sophie went on to write that James asked after his Aunt Beatrice and when she would return to Liverpool; that he played well with the baker's son, who was nearly the same age; and that he always put a bowl of milk out for the stray cat that had become a daily visitor. Beatrice had already sent to Aunt Sophie the first installment of the agreement with *his lordship*. The second hundred pounds was in the hands of Madame Devereux. If he was satisfied with the sennight, he would not request its return. The sum alone should have been a warning bell that he was to be no ordinary patron.

She bit down on her lower lip. She had considered putting an end to her whoring and finding employment as a governess or companion to an aging dowager. Her entrée into the Inn of the Red Chrysanthemum had been the means of ensnaring Nicholas and William Edelton, spoiled young men from a wealthy family. They thought they were entitled to anything and could do anything without reproach. They had no consideration for others. If not for their kind, her sister Charlotte might still be alive. James would have a mother. He would not have been born a bastard, the offspring of a travesty.

And society would provide no justice, would force no redress upon men of privilege. Thus, Beatrice had sought her own recompense. Nicholas and William would be punished for what they had done to her sister.

The door opened, startling her to her feet. For a second, she hoped it to be Allison, returned to rescue her. But it was *his lordship*.

"My cook had prepared a breakfast before he departed," he said as he placed a tray with coffee, toast, jam, egg, and ham upon the sideboard. "I suggest you partake heartily. You will require stamina."

Her heart pounded at the forewarning. She watched as he placed a large kettle of water above the fire. He then went to the armoire and looked through her modest collection of clothing.

"Did you leave your finer items at the Inn?" he asked.

His question reminded her of why she detested men of wealth. They acted and spoke as they pleased.

"My wardrobe is none of your concern," she replied, wanting to shut the door of the armoire in his face. She might have indulged in better clothes, but every pence she spent upon herself was one less for James.

He cocked a brow at her. "You've a stubborn penchant in you."

Against her better judgment, despite what he had said earlier, and though she had thought to make a lark of her time with the attractive stranger, she bristled. "No more than you possess, I'm sure."

No doubt he appreciated a stranger's assessment of him as little as she.

"And foolhardy to boot," he said, his tone dark and ominous.

If he was angry with her for what she had done to him last night, she wished he would simply own the fact. Instead, he went about with an eerie calm and restraint, save when he had threatened to flog her within an inch of her life. She did not think it an empty menace. She had overlooked the indications that this was to be no ordinary tryst, and her challenges to him earlier had shown *his lordship* intended no hoax. She had provoked something fierce when she had called him "my pet." The angry flash in his eyes could not have been counterfeit.

He looked down at her. "I thought harlots enjoyed decorating themselves with the spoils of their lovers."

She sucked in her breath. The man was insufferable. He disliked her, too. She was certain of it now. But why would he wish to pay a hundred pounds to bed a woman he abhorred? Why had he pleasured her in the library? But perhaps he had no intention of bedding her. What had he said of the screams ringing from the rafters? She wondered if he might be some evil character akin to the ones found in *Justine*. She was, in effect, his prisoner, with nowhere to go and no one to turn to. With no servants, she would have to rely upon him for everything.

"Am I a captive here?" she blurted.

"You are free to leave at any moment, Miss Primrose. You are hardly charming enough for me to risk being thrown in gaol on the charge of kidnapping."

She stared at him, mouth agape. Aside from being called a darkie, she had never been so offended.

"What binds you here is your own avarice," he said, stepping toward her. "You are a whore trading your wares for money. I fail to see any dilemma for you."

"If I decide to leave, where would I head?" she inquired, refusing to be intimidated by him.

He shrugged. "When you depart my property, you are no longer my concern."

She went to the sideboard, pretending to desire a cup of coffee, though her primary objective was to put more distance between them. Remembering how he had trapped her between the bookcase and his body, she scolded herself for having been aroused by him. She drank her coffee to give herself time to think.

"What is it you intend to do with me?" she asked, hoping her voice did not quiver as much as she felt.

"What does a whore such as yourself merit?"

"I am beginning to doubt that *your* charms are worth a hundred quid."

He grinned—in amusement, she thought. It was a brief moment of levity amidst grim discourse.

"Two hundred," he reminded her.

Two hundred pounds was a good sum, but was it worth a sennight with this strange and gloomy nobleman? She had no experience with the submissive role. From the start, she knew she wanted the dominant role and had been fortunate enough to learn under the tutelage of a woman named Mistress Scarlet. Knowing what she had inflicted upon others, she wondered that she could withstand being the recipient. She suddenly had a newfound appreciation for those who took on the part of submission.

*****

Spencer watched Miss Primrose drink her coffee. She had not responded and seemed to be contemplating whether to accept his proposal. He wanted to tell her she had already done so, but he had also said she was free to leave. She had a right to reconsider her decision, which vexed him because she had already gotten him to double his initial offering. If the trollop thought she could exploit more from him…it would be a feat if he did not strangle her before the sennight was over.

He saw her glance in the direction of the writing table before she finished her coffee. She looked at the food upon the tray but took nothing.

"Eat," he said.

Her back stiffened. He wondered if she would ever settle into the role of a submissive one, but it mattered not to him. She picked up the fork and poked at the ham.

"This is a great deal more than I am accustomed to for breakfast," she said, putting down the fork.

He folded his arms. "Given your exertions last night, I would have anticipated you to have a voracious appetite."

She lifted her chin, then smiled. "Did you enjoy the, er, performance?"

He clenched his jaw. *Teasing, brazen hussy.*

"Careful, Miss Primrose," he said. "I would not advise playing with fire. Allow me to dissuade you from contemplating another *performance* of its kind. I will not speak to my enjoyment last night, but I assuredly will enjoy giving *you* a fair turn."

He had the satisfaction of seeing her smile dissipate and her eyes widen.

"If you wish to go hungry," he continued, "that is your privilege. There is no further repast until the noon hour."

The cover on the kettle rattled from the boiling water inside. Steam rose from the openings. He went to retrieve the kettle, noticing, from the corner of his eye, Miss Primrose pick up the toast grudgingly. Taking the kettle to the cast iron tub in the closet adjoining the dressing room, he mixed the scalding water with tepid water from the pitcher. He hung linen upon the folding screens and set a small table of salts and soaps beside the tub.

When he returned, Miss Primrose was chewing her toast as if she were being forced to eat sand. She was looking again in the direction of the writing table.

"Your bath is ready," he announced.

She finished her toast. He could sense her ambivalence. No doubt she wanted the money, but she had expected to be in command. The turn of events was clearly not to her liking.

They stood facing each other in silence for a moment before she arched a brow and said, "If you insist upon assuming the duties of my abigail, I shall require some assistance with this corset."

Lifting her curls atop her head, she turned her back to him. He'd had had a good visual of her back last night as she rode his cock, having straddled him in reverse. His cock stirred again. Taking a deep breath through his nose to calm the desire springing to life in his veins, he sauntered over to her and examined the lacing of the corset. He had unlaced stays before, but he feared if he undid hers, he might be tempted to do more than undress her. He had to prove he was in control.

But if she was to take a bath, she had to disrobe. Best to finish the task quickly with as little contact as possible. He untied the end of the ribbon and pulled it through the first grommet. She shifted, and her rump seemed to protrude closer toward him. The blood pounded in his head. He could see its shape beneath the thin shift. His hands itched to palm the fleshy enticement, the buttocks full enough for him to sink his fingers into. Forcing his gaze back to the corset, he began to unwind the ribbon. The damn thing would not move fast enough for him.

Her proximity had a disconcerting effect upon him, and relief flooded him when, at last, he had the intolerable thing unlaced. He took several steps back and allowed her to slip the corset off herself, swallowing with difficulty as he discerned the silhouette of her body through the thin muslin of her shift. The blood throbbed in his groin.

"Your bath is ready," he said again, a little hoarsely.

"Will you be assisting with the bathing?" she asked as she held out her corset for him.

He groaned inwardly at the temptation. "Do you require assistance?"

She thought for a moment before replying, "No."

Relieved, he watched her enter the closet and close the door behind her. He put the corset upon a chair, half wondering how one laundered the stiff undergarment, and returned to the armoire. She had but three gowns, and they were all ordinary. With the money she had procured from Nicholas and William, she could have afforded much finer dresses. And the petticoats he saw had been mended in several places. For a moment, he opted for no clothing at all. From what Mr. Fields had described, she often had

Nicholas and William parade about without a shred of clothing. But a sennight—six days now—was plenty of time. He intended to put Miss Primrose through her paces within reason. He pulled out a simple muslin whose aurulent color had faded into an ecru, short stays, a shift, and petticoats.

He searched the drawers for garters and petticoats but came across a black velvet pouch first. Curious, he emptied the contents into one hand. Various metal items fell out. One of them bore the shape of the number eight—a smaller circle joined to a larger circle. His blood boiled as he recalled one particularly difficult letter to read. Mr. Fields had written:

Mistress Primrose applies a pair of rings to Mr. William's cock. The larger of the circles fits about the base of his cock. As it is still soft, the top of the shaft fits easily through the smaller circle. She strokes him and cradles his sack with her hand. Soon his cock grows hard, but it is trapped in the rings and cannot lengthen into its natural state of erection. Instead, the cock is forced into a strange contortion, like the body of a snake. In this state, she fondles him and teases him with the sight of her own body. Mr. William whimpers and begins to beg.

Did Miss Primrose intend to use this device upon him? Spencer wondered angrily. In disgust, he threw the items back into their pouch. He glanced at the door to the closet, irritated that she was not yet done. He strode over with the intent of throwing open the door.

*****

The embrace of hot water felt heavenly against her skin. Beatrice nestled as far as she could into the tub. What a luxury to be able to recline in the bath! She had poured some of the scented oils upon the table into the water. The smell of lavender curled with the steam into her nose. She had also found a small bottle of lotion "for use in the treatment of *champi*." She applied it to her hair. It produced a much better lather than soap. She leaned back till the water washed over her hair, forgetting her predicament for the moment. She sat up and smoothed back her wet hair, feeling more refreshed than she could remember.

But what to do with *his lordship*? She did not want to accept his terms, but what else could she do if she wanted the other hundred quid? The man baffled her. He seemed to desire and detest her all at once, though she suffered the same paradox concerning him. He also seemed angry at her, and apart from what she had done to him last night, she could not fathom why.

She drew the sponge languidly along her arm. He was quite the delectable sight tied to the bedposts. His chest was lovely to the touch. And his cock…the perfect length and thickness. She shivered at the memory of how it had felt inside of her, how forcefully he had bucked his hips at her, his endurance and determination to spend.

The sponge grazed her erect nipple. She slipped her hand between her thighs. Her muscles were sore, but her cunnie eager to be filled by him. She closed her eyes. How could she want this man? Had she been so deprived, her lust suppressed, while pursuing her vengeance against Nicholas and William that she would welcome a vexatious, disdainful nobleman between her legs? Could she be swayed by a handsome face? Or was it the promise of his abilities in the boudoir, the skillful touch that he had shown in the library, that drew her?

She started to see him there, leaning against the doorframe. She sat up, only to discover in doing so, her breasts came above the water. She quickly crossed her arms in front of her. How long had the man been standing there? Had he observed her touching herself? Her cheeks grew hot.

"I am not yet finished with the bath," she said.

"Yes, you are."

The intensity of his stare would have melted ice. He walked over and pulled the towel off the folding screen. He held it open for her.

"I am quite capable of drying myself," she insisted.

"Come, Miss Primrose. Modesty in a whore is unnecessary."

Beatrice clenched her teeth. The man needed a good walloping.

"I can see why a man of your sort must need resort to being a gap stopper. Your charms could not persuade a hedge whore to your bed."

They stared at one another. Neither blinked.

"I can wait all day," he said at last.

She bristled. The heat of the water had waned. The skin upon her fingers had begun to wrinkle.

"I would rather not, however," he added. "You are free to use the drip method for drying."

She sucked in her breath. "You're an insufferable var—"

"How best to discipline an unruly submissive one?" he wondered aloud.

Suppressing a scowl, she rose to her feet. She put a hand in front of her crotch and crossed her other arm over her breasts. Despite the awkward sensation that she was on display, she decided she did not want to give him the satisfaction of knowing how much he irked her. Instead of hastily reaching for the towel, she allowed him to drink in the sight of her.

He stared at her nakedness. His gaze took in her belly, her

hips, her legs, and the breasts she covered. The towel he held concealed any evidence that he was visibly aroused *there*, but she saw his eyes dilate with lust.

"Step out," he ordered.

She did as told. He wrapped the towel about her and began to dry her arms and her back. He worked his way down, patting her buttocks with the towel and dragging it down one leg than the other. Without a word, she submitted to the task, feeling like a child who could not be trusted to dry herself.

"Place your hands at your sides," he said.

She dropped her arms, which failed to conceal much in any case.

He dried the inside of her legs. The towel grazed the intimate folds between her thighs. He moved the towel over her abdomen, her belly button, and onto her breasts. Her nipples perked at the contact. He took a step back and looked her over from head to toe. He had neglected to dry her hair first, and water trickled in little rivulets down her body. His smoldering stare had a stimulating effect, and her discomfort increased with a distressing arousal. Knowing that he was not simply a lascivious lecher wont to ogle women but a man who seemed to dislike her with surprising intensity, his desire empowered her.

Reaching out, he cradled the bottom of one breast. His touch sent prickles throughout her. He eyed her areola, and she thought he might try to capture the nipple in his mouth. He brushed a thumb over it, and she inadvertently moaned. She recalled how she had tormented his nipple last night, how she had licked, bit, and suckled that sensitive bud. He had said he intended to repay her in kind. She braced herself for what was to come.

But he released her breast and stood back once more.

"Touch yourself."

The words, a little raspy from his lust, echoed in her ears. Ambivalence stayed her. She was no stranger to touching herself to excite a man, but it had always been at her initiative. A command performance was another matter.

"Do not make me repeat myself, Miss Primrose."

After a relenting sigh, she cupped both her breasts.

"Fondle them," he ordered.

She kneaded them in circles, pressing the orbs together, higher, and apart. This time she could see the stiffness at his crotch. The wantonness began to challenge the embarrassment of such an exhibition, causing a warm sensation to build between her legs.

"Now your teats."

The hunger in his eyes made her feel heady, and she almost smirked with satisfaction. Was he in as much control as he thought? She rolled her nipples between her thumbs and fore-fingers, making them protrude further. She pulled at them and groaned. He took one of her hands and moved it to the patch of curls at the base of her pelvis.

"Pleasure yourself."

She hesitated, but then obliged by sliding two fingers between her thighs, pressing them into her folds. A familiar dampness emerged there. Of her own volition, she continued to roll and squeeze her breast with the other hand. Distracted by her own caresses, she barely noticed him tossing the towel onto a chair before unbuttoning his coat. The drops of water upon her body had turned cold, but the heat inside her womanhood had grown.

After several minutes, he ordered her to stop. He had removed his coat and opened the fall of his pants and smallclothes. His cock stood gloriously erect. She greeted it with anticipation, remembering how full it had felt inside of her. He stroked himself.

"On your knees, Miss Primrose."

His voice quivered. She knew what he wanted. A part of her wanted very much to taste him. A man could be quite vulnerable entrusting his precious organ to a woman's mouth. But she knew many who deemed the act of cock sucking debasing, the ultimate task of a lowly whore. Suspecting *his lordship* to agree with the latter sentiment, she recoiled at the idea of submitting to this entitled rogue.

"A hundred pounds is at stake," he reminded her.

Gritting her teeth, she knelt before him. He pointed the head of his cock at her mouth. Reluctantly, she parted her lips. She licked the underside of his shaft, then circled her tongue about the tip. He groaned his reception. She wrapped a hand around his hardness. Perhaps she could distract him and make him spend by hand and not have to take him into her orifice. With her forefinger, she drew the liquid that had seeped from the top of his cock down to a sensitive spot just below the head. Then she pumped her hand up and down the rod of velvet and steel.

He allowed her to work his cock with her hand for several minutes, but, sensing her avoidance, he said, "Take it into your mouth."

She gripped his cock hard and grudgingly applied her mouth to the head.

"More," he grunted.

He groaned as his cock slid along her tongue, further into her mouth. She stayed there with his cock pulsing inside her. He fisted his hand in her hair and drew her head closer to him until his whole length was encased, the hair at his pelvis tickling her nose. She began to gag. Her body heaved as if needing to retch. His hand remained firm against the back of her head, and she forced herself to relax, hoping he would spend soon.

At a leisurely pace, he maneuvered her head up and down his shaft. She felt its tip hit the back of her throat several times. Wanting to finish him off, she sucked at the cock, pumping in and out of her mouth. His eyes widened.

"Mother of God," he breathed.

He shoved his hips at her more quickly. Inspired by her own abilities, she sucked him harder and made sure her tongue rubbed against him with every thrust. His muscles tensed. The veins in his neck protruded. She did her best to keep up and not lose her focus or she would find herself gagging once more as he fucked her mouth with increasing ferocity. At last, with a roar, he began to convulse. She felt thick, hot liquid filling her mouth. She sputtered but was stymied by his hold upon her head, pressing her face into his pelvis.

When he had pumped the last of his seed into her mouth, he released her and stumbled back. The tang of his semen still upon her tongue, she vacillated between hating the man and feeling victorious. The arousal from her earlier ministrations upon herself had not completely dissipated, and she considered what she might do to bring his cock to life again.

"Satisfied?" she asked archly, attempting to stoke her triumph.

He only stared at her. With some disappointment, she watched him replace his fall. He adjusted his neckcloth and picked up his coat.

She rose to her feet with a sigh. "May I have the towel?"

He handed it to her, and she wrapped it about her body. Without a backward glance, she walked by him. She would stay for the money, she decided. But there had to be a way she could gain control of the situation.

*****

Spencer shuddered. The sight of her thick lips wrapped about his cock would have been enough to send him over the edge. The warm wetness of her mouth surrounding his cock, the pressure of her sucking, the tip of his penis grazing her throat were all nothing short of marvelous. He felt a little remorse at having held her head so tightly the times she appeared to choke, but she had regained control well enough.

The vision of her naked and wet danced in his mind. Unlike the skinny strumpets that had serviced him, Miss Primrose had a roundness to her that he found attractive. The curve of her arse, in particular. He had palmed its fullness through the towel when drying her. She was not malnourished, which spoke again to her station in life. He wondered what had caused her to fall from grace and wind up at the Inn of the Red Chrysanthemum?

He would have to have her bathe more often, he decided. The water sliding down the swell of a breast, down the plane of her belly to the damp curls above her cunnie was worthy of a painting. He wondered how she considered the fellatio. Did she find it degrading or enjoyable or was she ambivalent? He reminded himself not to care. He followed her into the main chamber and found she had replaced her towel with a banyan. Her brow furrowed and she looked about the room in disconcertion.

"I require the services of an abigail," she snapped.

Feeling relaxed, he took no offense at her tone and said almost jovially, "I am at your disposal."

She glared at him. "For a private matter."

He raised his brows. "More private than a bath?"

She squirmed, and he finally realized what she required. "Ah, the chamber pot."

He retrieved a commode made of china. She looked horrified.

"I will tend to it later," she mumbled.

"As you wish."

He set the chamber pot aside and watched her pick up her shift. She hesitated.

"Do you not have other affairs to tend to?" she asked.

She had stood before him naked as a newborn babe but minutes ago but now found it distressing to dress before him?

"Allow me," he said, taking devious delight in her dismay as he approached her.

Standing behind her, he slid the robe down her shoulders. He kissed the exposed body part and thought he felt her quiver. He brushed aside her hair and kissed her neck. As he continued to plant light kisses along her neck and shoulders, he wrapped his left arm around her and grasped her right breast. She let out a shaky breath. He felt the nipple harden beneath his palm. She had lovely brown areolas, each as large as a cartwheel twopence. He dug his fingers into the pliant flesh as his other arm snaked around her hip. He worked his hand between her thighs and found dampness there.

"My God, you're wet," he remarked, sliding his fingers along her slit.

She gasped when he grazed her clitoris.

"Do you wish to spend, Miss Primrose?" he asked softly in her ear.

She moaned as he inserted a finger into her cunnie, gathered the nectar there, and spread it upon the swollen nub nestled between her folds.

"Do you?" he repeated, fondling her in earnest.

"Yes."

"Good. Perhaps you will have the chance to earn it."

He pinched the nipple playfully before withdrawing his hands. He stepped away from her.

"For now, let us finish your toilette," he said, enjoying her crestfallen look.

He had not viewed his sennight with Miss Primrose with eagerness. He saw his vengeance, especially crafted for her, as a chore. But now he believed he could take great pleasure in punishing Miss Primrose and enjoy every minute.

PART IV

Punishing Miss Primrose

PUNISHING MISS PRIMROSE, PART IV

"IT IS QUITE unnecessary for you to be here while I dress," Beatrice Primrose said with her best attempt at nonchalance though she was seething inside.

His lordship, as he insisted upon being called and as he had not provided her his name, sat in a chair next to the sideboard and reached for a slice of toast from her unfinished breakfast upon the tray.

"What if you were to require my assistance?" he asked unconcerned, as he crossed one long leg over the other.

Dressed in fresh linen, a waistcoat of striped brocade, his collar starched, his cravat crisply tied, and his boots shined to a gloss, he had the appearance of a gentleman, but Beatrice had determined he was far from gentlemanly. A gentleman would not have aroused her, fondling her in her most private place, then walked away and commanded her to finish dressing, leaving her bereft and agitated. She pulled her banyan tighter about her, vexed at herself for having desired him and finding him the least bit attractive. His lovely, light brown locks waving above a handsome countenance might persuade most women, but his charms were decidedly lacking.

"I shall not," she answered.

He chewed the toast, swallowed, and said, "If you insist."

Instead of budging, he helped himself to another slice of toast and began to butter it. She wanted to scream at him to leave the boudoir but suspected he was enjoying her discomfiture. The additional hundred quid that she would receive from completing her sojourn with the insufferable nobleman sitting beside the sideboard would relieve her from her current arrangement with Madame Devereux of the Inn of the Red Chrysanthemum, but she now wondered if the money was worth the effort. She wondered that she could last the required sennight with him. She had arrived at his estate but yesterday.

With an exasperated sigh, she let the robe fall from her and quickly put on the shift he had laid out upon the bed. He had already seen her naked in the bath. It was a bit silly of her to mind his witness now. She shoved aside the memory of his strong hands upon her as he dried her with a towel. She shrugged into the short stays, grateful that they laced in front and did not require his assistance. The madman had sent away all the servants, including her maid. She tried not to let his remark about *screams ringing from the rafters* trouble her. Glancing toward him, she saw that he had ceased buttering the bread. He looked at her with that familiar heat in his eyes. His lashes were nearly as long and full as hers.

She supposed her situation could be worse. For a lot less than a hundred quid, she could be faced with an ugly, old, smelly, foul, corpulent patron instead of a rugged member of polite society. But privileged men had no modesty and no scruples. They believed their place in society gave them *carte blanche* to do as they wished with no regard to others. At the Inn of the Red Chrysanthemum, where members explored the erotic in its most extreme forms, she had always assumed the dominant role to her submissive counterparts, and she derived a certain amount of satisfaction from putting wealthy, cosseted men in their place. When she had agreed to spend a sennight with *his lordship*, she had thought to be reprising her role as the dominant one.

But he had intended differently.

She tied her petticoats, then yelped as she attempted to pin her gown together.

"In need of assistance?"

"Dressed a great many women, have you?" she challenged. "You must be quite a man-of-the-town."

He made no answer, merely replacing the butter knife and brushed the bread crumbs from his thighs.

"You are not required to be dressed, Miss Primrose. I have no qualms should you wish to walk about *sans* clothing."

She ground her teeth. Insufferable man. She would be glad to be done with him and the Red Chrysanthemum. The Inn had served her purpose as the venue for her revenge upon Nicholas and William Edelton. She had exacted a dear sum between the two, though no amount of money could replace the sister she had lost. The letter from her aunt lay upon the writing table, a reminder of her purpose, the worthy pursuit of her ignoble deeds. After this final business with *his lordship*, she would return to Liverpool, to her aunt and James, find suitable employment, and hopefully never have to deal with a rich bastard again.

What upset her most about her current situation with *his lordship* was the betrayal of her own body. It *would* respond to him. She could feel the humidity between her legs still, and the last thing she wanted was to layer on more garments. She wanted to spend, as she had in his bed, his cock buried deep inside her. The salve she had used upon him could not have worked better, allowing her to ride him for as long as she needed. Only after her third orgasm did he finally find release. The memory of their perspiring bodies rocking the bed made the heat pulse low and deep within her.

She had an inspiration.

His lordship needed to be taught a lesson. In the course of less than four and twenty hours, he had disparaged her charms and called her a whore several times. If she was to spend a sennight with him, she need not allow him free rein to lord over her as he had done, to condescend and insult her with impunity. He may hold all the cards, but she would show him that he was as weak as any other mortal man. That he harbored little fondness for her would only make her triumph more significant and fulfilling.

*****

Spencer Edelton, the Marquess of Carey, knew not why he ate her toast when he had partaken of his own breakfast not two hours before.

No, he did know.

The food provided a convenient distraction from Miss Primrose. The image of her naked and wet from the bath haunted him, and the thrill from the fellatio she had performed afterwards had not completely dissipated from his body. Her supple lips wrapped about him, her cheeks caved inward as she sucked, her tongue rubbing against the underside of his shaft, the warmth, the wetness all conspired to a rapturous indulgence of the senses. He could have spent within minutes but battled himself to prolong the bliss.

He looked over her breakfast tray. She should eat more. Though she had more flesh upon her than most common trollops—he reminded himself that she was no slattern for she had exhorted a great deal of money from his brother and cousin—she would require more sustenance than the coffee and single slice of toast he had seen her consume. Perhaps he should cease vexing her. A reprieve might allow her to attend to her appetite.

But she was a grown woman—a few years past twenty, he suspected. And he should not care if she wished to starve herself. His purpose in tolerating and paying for her company was to provide her an unforgettable set-down. To repay pain with pain. Yet despite what she had done to his cousin, William, and in particular his brother, Nicholas, Spencer doubted he could be as malicious as she. And that doubt angered him. She deserved a great deal worse than what he had in store for her. For the first time ever, he considered his inadequate villainy a failing. He would, however, attempt his best.

"You should have one of the eggs and a slice of ham," he said.

"Thank you, but I had a mouthful of cockmeat and a dram of mettle earlier," she replied as she continued to apply the pins to her dress.

He shifted in his chair. While the quality of her speech suggested her upbringing was not one of poverty or neglect, she had, at times, a most vulgar tongue. Her aplomb lessened the crudeness of her words, and, to his own surprise, he found the incongruous blend in her speech provocative. She was capable of fine manners, as he had witnessed at dinner last evening, and a few of her remarks in the library evidenced her intelligence and showed even the aptitude for philosophy. It was a shame she had fallen into such a disreputable situation in life.

He caught himself. It was a shame she was a ruinous doxy. She was a menace, draining the purses and souls of the men she seduced into her clutches. His uncle had taken Nicholas and William to Belgium, and Spencer hoped the change of scene would dispel his brother's despondency. How Miss Primrose had ensnared such devotion from Nicholas he could not understand.

Nicholas, with his golden locks and winning smile, could have had any number of ladies of the *ton*. Why had he tossed discretion to the wind and poured his heart and purse strings to a whore who beat and whipped him?

"If you wish to be of use," Miss Primrose said, approaching him, "you may assist with my garters."

She handed him the ribbons, then pulled up her skirts and propped her left foot upon his right knee. He started. The last time she had initiated contact, his cock had been hard for over an hour. Her skirts slid past her raised knee and down her thigh. She had shapely legs. Not the thin twigs he saw on most strumpets. He calmed his quickened pulse as he slipped the stocking upon her, his fingers grazing her near hairless leg. He wound the ribbon below her knee, wondering that she did not possess a pair of spring garters. Where was the evidence of the money she had fleeced from Nicholas and William? It was not possible she could have wasted it all away at the card tables or in drink. He remembered a passing reference to a man named James—her lover, no doubt. Perhaps the pair meant to flee the country and spend their spoils in Scotland or France. His anger rose at her duplicity. Poor Nicholas. In his last letter to her, he had begged to be allowed to return to her, writing that his soul would be forever lost in winter without her summer rays. Likely he had not known that Miss Primrose entertained another man's affections.

When he had finished one leg, instead of replacing her foot where she stood, she brought it down upon the opposite side of his leg and momentarily straddled his knees before transferring her weight to her left leg and placing her right foot upon his left knee. His heart rate soared. Did she know her effect upon him? He would call upon his anger to stymie the desire she aroused in him, but it seemed his antagonism was as likely to fuel his lust than not. Affecting indifference, he proceeded to tie her other stocking with the garter. Perhaps he had erred in dismissing the servants, but he could not risk alarming them. He would have confined his plans to the Inn at the Red Chrysanthemum, but he did not want Miss Primrose to have an easy escape.

"Your slippers are—" he began after tying the remaining garter.

She slid onto his knees once more and leaned toward him.

"If I am to agree to stay the duration of the sennight," she said, "it is only fair that I know what you intend with me."

"What more do you need know? I thought I made it quite clear how it is to be here."

Her arse shifted past his knees, and he could feel the blood churning once more in his groin. He had already spent, gloriously, in her mouth. Yet his cock was stirring to life as if it were starved.

"Have you much experience in the role of the dominant one?" she asked, bracing against the arms of the chair, subtly arching her back. He had an ample visual of her bosom. The memory of her large brown areolas filled his mind.

"Sufficient for our purposes," he replied.

"I am new to the submissive position," she said, adjusting his neckcloth. "I hope you will be forgiving of my inexperience."

His body grew hot. "I will show the same mercy you have shown to your submissive ones."

She raised a brow. "What do you know of my forbearance?"

Revealing his relation to Nicholas would scare her. He had not been able to hide his enmity, and she was no fool.

"Your ways are not unknown, Mistress Primrose," he deflected, then cursed himself.

"I do like the sound of my name upon your lips," she said, her voice sultry in triumph.

One of her hands dropped below his waist, reaching for his cock, but he caught her by the wrist. He did not like the influence this temptress had upon him.

"A slip of the tongue," he said. "It shall not happen again."

"You may find you enjoy me better as Mistress Primrose."

The muscle along his jaw tightened. "I think not."

"I vow I have never had any complaints to the contrary."

Her other hand reached between his legs, but he grabbed that wrist, too. He held her hands together in front of her. Her bosom swelled. She pinned him with a sensual stare.

"Allow me to demonstrate a little of what I am capable of as Mistress."

"You've shown me enough," he growled, recalling how she had tormented him in his bed last night.

"Did you not enjoy being in my mouth? If you please me, perhaps you shall be rewarded with an encore."

He shook his head in disbelief and regard for her perseverance. "You will persist in the notion that you are Mistress?"

"It is all I know."

"If I could ever contemplate submitting to anyone—and I doubt I have the nature for it—I would certainly not yield to you."

"The nature? You would be surprised, your lordship, with the sort of men who have passed through the doors of the Red Chrysanthemum. Commanding generals, dictating magistrates, men of influence and power have all readily knelt in submission before a dominant one. There is no shame. You need not fear it."

"Fear? You think me afraid?"

"Yes, but I assure you a proper Mistress will care for her submissive one. It is the responsibility of the dominant one to provide the greatest of pleasure, sometimes through pain because it can enhance pleasure. But an experienced dominant one will know the limitations of her partner. As a Mistress, I take this responsibility seriously."

"How noble of you," he replied drily. "And you've shown such consideration to all your victims?"

Her back straightened at his inflammatory choice in words. He had intended his question as a statement, for he doubted she cared in the least for Nicholas or William. The more he thought of her duplicity, the more incensed he became.

"The men come to me, of their own free will, because they *want* to," she declared.

"Because you deceive them."

"Were *you* deceived? Did you not willingly request me?" Her voice dropped half an octave. "Is it not because you *desired* me?"

He wanted to throw her from his lap, but could not. Despite his anger, he knew the truth of her implication. How was it he could desire this wicked hussy? Was lust so much more powerful than intellect?

No, he would not be tempted by her. Not now. Not before he had dissuaded her that she had any hold or control upon him. The very idea of submitting to her was repulsive enough.

"Though you despise me, yet you desire me," she said. "Perhaps you consider it degrading to lie with a whore, a whore of my...sort. I have not the alabaster skin and refined manners of the women of the *ton*. But you are titillated by my difference, my inferior situation."

He stared at her, wondering if what she said might be true.

She lowered her mouth toward his hands, which still gripped her wrists. "My cunnie, my mouth, felt as sweet as any upon your cock, eh?"

She slid her tongue beneath his smallest finger, caught it between her teeth, and gently pulled it into her mouth. She sucked it, and he was immediately reminded of how her mouth felt about his cock.

"Enough," he said, throwing her hands aside. Hell and damnation. He would have thought himself to possess more forbearance than he felt. Unlike the members of the crew aboard the third rate, he had not sought out a whorehouse the instant the ship pulled into a port. He had refused many women who threw themselves at him. Why could he not remain indifferent to Miss Primrose?

He moved as if to rise from the chair, but she remained where she was and braced herself against the gilded arms of the chair. Leaning forward, she whispered beside his ear.

"Fuck me."

*****

His eyes had widened, and Beatrice heard a surrendering groan. She straightened, but before she could read the effect of her words upon his features, he had pressed a hand to the back of her head and crushed her mouth down to his. His lips devoured hers with a vehemence that made her head spin. She could hardly catch her breath, let alone celebrate her conquest. The man may have thought himself in control, may have wished to fill the role of a dominant one, but when it came to carnal matters, all men were weak.

His breath was warm and heavy upon her as he took large mouthfuls of her lips. Power was an aphrodisiac, and her ability to excite such a strong desire in him made her heady with victory. She returned his bruising kiss, delving her tongue into his hot, wet mouth. With both hands, she grasped his head, holding him in place so that she could manipulate her tongue all around his oral orifice. He relinquished his hold of her head and grasped her legs, trying to pull her farther upon his lap, but the arms of the chair proved an impediment. She could have thrown her legs over the arms, but she wanted him to wait as their tongues danced and dueled. She pulled upon his lower lip with her teeth, then trailed her tongue along his jaw before nipping at his earlobe.

Her hands made quick work of his neckcloth. His hands sought her breasts, but she wanted to dictate the course of action. She pressed her mouth against his neck, seeking its most tender areas, working her tongue upon the softness beneath his jaw and the indent at the base of his neck. He grunted and shifted in the chair. She latched on to the side of his neck and sucked with increasing vigor while her hands undid his fall. As expected, his cock was hard as steel by now. She held it tight, its thickness the perfect size for her hand. She wanted it inside her, but first she would prolong the anticipation so that he fully appreciated his own desperation.

"You desire me something fierce, *your lordship*," she remarked, finding the moisture at the tip of his cock and spreading it along his length.

He shivered. She pumped her hand up and down a few times, then took his hands and placed them upon her breasts. He grabbed them and moved his thumbs over the area of her nipples. She closed her eyes and moaned, feeling the buds harden beneath his touch. Pulling her skirts higher, she lifted her legs over the arms of the chair and moved herself closer to his pelvis. She held on to the back of the chair.

"Tell me how much you desire me," she said, pushing herself against his cock.

"Impudent doxy," he returned.

She moved back. "Tell me."

"I would rather show you."

He grabbed her by the hips and pulled her to his erection. He ground himself at her as if to pierce the layers of skirt between them.

"Does it dismay you to crave a lowly whore?" she asked, but received only an intense stare from him.

Undaunted, she continued, "I find that men who present themselves as upright citizens and worthy gentlemen hide a most naughty penchant. You mentioned Cleopatra once. Is it a bawdy dream of yours to fuck the Queen of Egypt? Do you wish to play the part of Antony to me?"

He tightened his hold upon her and moved her more vigorously atop him. "I would sooner play the part of Octavius."

She frowned, remembering Octavius to be the Roman Emperor seeking Cleopatra's surrender and his intent to parade her through Rome at his triumph. The pleasurable effect produced by the friction of the fabric against her cunnie stalled her annoyance.

"I do not think Octavius had the privilege of Cleopatra's favors," she returned.

His lordship slid his hand beneath her skirts and found his way to her womanhood, where he strummed his thumb along the nub of flesh between her thighs.

"I would not suit the part of Antony, but you would make a fitting Cleopatra."

Again she frowned, understanding him to intend an insult more than praise. Yesterday he had likened her to Moll Flanders. But his stroking kept her vexation at bay. She parted her legs wider. He dipped his thumb into her wetness and coated her clitoris with it. Ripples of delight fanned from that sensitive little flesh.

"But if you were to be Octavius," she said, "I wonder that Cleopatra would be the one submitting in the end?"

She grasped his cock and rubbed the sensitive underside furiously. He groaned. His patience evaporated, and he threw up her skirts.

"Wait!" she gasped.

She fumbled for the pocket in her skirts and pulled out a condom. He barely waited for her to finish tying it upon his shaft before lifting her and thrusting all of him into her. She cried out at being filled so deeply all at once, though her wetness allowed him to slide in with relative ease. His lashes rested against his cheeks as he soaked up the pleasure of her impaled upon his cock. She felt it throb against the walls of her cunnie. For a moment she regretted not reaching for the salve she had applied to him last night. He might not last long enough for her to achieve her climax.

"Are you close to spending?" she asked. "Are you capable of lasting longer or will you sputter as quickly as a little boy?"

He stared at her and bucked his hips at her hard. Her challenge succeeded for he pummeled his cock in and out of her for some time. Her awkward position in the chair made it difficult for her to aid his efforts, but he responded well to her cues, her moans of pleasure and her gasps of delight, and positioned himself so that she could grind herself against his pelvis. She was glad for his strength as he lifted her effortlessly and brought her down upon his cock again and again and again. Hot tension built inside her, reaching to the ends of her limbs. Her cries grew louder and faster. He thrust into her with such rapidity she thought her teeth would clatter.

Her climax erupted over her, making her shudder and jerk against him. He pounded into her several times and achieved his own orgasm. She felt a surge of heat in her cunnie and his cock pulsing. Her heart hammered in her ears, and she thought she could hear the thudding of his. The room was silent but for their panting, synchronized for a few seconds before diverging in their own rhythms.

It mattered not if he wished to be Mark Antony or Octavius Caesar. Cleopatra would rule the day.

Satisfied and satiated, she admired the fine lines of his physiognomy. Perspiration beaded along his forehead.

"Well done, my pet," she praised.

It was too late. The words had slipped from her mouth before she could stop them. And from the way he now glared at her, she could see that he had not forgotten his warning to her.

*****

His body recoiled at the term. Had he not told her that he would be tempted to whip her within an inch of her life if she dared address him with that foul endearment she used for Nicholas and her other submissive quarries?

Spencer rose to his feet sharply but caught her by the arm before she tumbled to the ground. He dragged her, stumbling, over to the bed and thrust her against it.

"Undress yourself," he ordered as he ripped the sheath off his cock and took out his handkerchief to wipe himself.

"Your pardon, I misspoke," she said.

"I said *undress yourself.*"

His voice trembled with fury. Thoughts of making her beg for mercy—as she had demanded from Nicholas and William several times—raced through his mind. From what Mr. Fields, the Bow Street Runner he had hired to follow Nicholas, described, Miss Primrose had spared little and infrequent mercy to the younger Edelton, and only after much torment and torture. Why had he even allowed her to spend just now, Spencer wondered. He could have easily taken his own pleasure and left her unfulfilled. That would teach her to use her wiles upon him.

"But I just completed dressing," she protested with a nervous laugh.

He felt the veins at his temple pulse. "Do you wish me to rip the clothing from you?"

With a deep breath, she carefully began to unpin her gown. He tossed the prophylactic into the chamber pot and replaced his fall. While she slid her outer garments from her and placed them upon the bed, he unbuttoned and divested himself of his coat. He watched her step out of her petticoats. She placed those upon the bed as well, then turned to face him for approval. He shook his head for she looked damned fetching in her stays and shift. The words of Domitius Enobarbus, Antony's lieutenant, echoed in his head:

Age cannot wither her, nor custom stale
Her infinite variety: other women cloy
The appetites they feed: but she makes hungry
Where most she satisfies; for vilest things
Become themselves in her: that the holy priests
Bless her when she is riggish.

Gathering his anger, he began formulating what he was to do. The morning had not gone as he had planned, but he was coming to the conclusion that he would have to think on his feet where Miss Primrose was concerned.

"Finish the task," he told her as he unwound the neckcloth she had loosened and tossed his collar.

He could see her mind turning, wondering what he intended, but too proud to ask. With slow hands, she unlaced her stays. He undid the cuffs of his sleeves, which seemed to alarm her a little. She stopped. He strode over to her and yanked the ribbon from her stays. She tensed at his anger, but his mind was awash with the reports Mr. Fields had provided, of Nicholas and William, often naked, pleading for forgiveness from her, acquiescing to her most outlandish demands while she addressed them—and treated them—as pets. William had once upset her somehow and was made to wear a woman's garments—stays, petticoats, stockings, and garters—and crawl upon the ground while she flogged him.

"Discard your shift," he said between gritted teeth.

She complied more promptly this time. The garment pooled at her feet. She had many curves to her body, all in a manner to entice. His gaze fell to the dark curls above her womanhood. To his amazement, he felt his hunger rise.

"Face the bedpost."

She turned to the one behind her. He grabbed her wrists and pinned them above her head. Using his neckcloth, he tied her hands to the bedpost. He stepped back and was instantly greeted by the sight of her pert and rounded rump. Naked but for her stockings and garters, she looked far too titillating tied to the bedpost. He cursed himself. Would he have to cut off his cock to refrain from being aroused by her?

Standing behind her, he wrapped his forearm around her hip and reached his hand between her thighs. She was sodden. He slid his fingers along her slit, making her moan.

"What a lascivious harlot," he said as he continued to rub her.

"The better to pleasure you, *your lordship.*"

"Do not think you will escape punishment by mending your behavior now. The deed is done. I have been tolerant and generous with you ere now."

He reached his other arm around her and tweaked her nipple.

Remembering how she had tormented his last night, relentlessly sucking and biting, he pinched her harder. She gasped. He palmed the breast. The orb was more than a handful. He squeezed its fullness, catching the nipple between his middle and forefinger. She made a low groan, and it seemed she had become wetter between the thighs. He was surprised the prospect of punishment had not damped her arousal. To be sure, he rolled and pinched her nipple between his thumb and forefinger. He mirrored the ministrations between her legs with her clitoris. Despite being tightly bound to the bedpost, she began to writhe in his hands. He intensified his fondling till he sensed she had reached that plane of agitation from which retreat would be agony.

The bedpost cleaved her breasts nicely, and he decided to grab them both. He tugged at both nipples, though his one hand, covered in the nectar of her desire, slipped off the pert little bud. He cupped the undersides of her breasts and brushed his thumbs over her hardened nipples. She groaned at the displacement of his hand, her hips wiggling at the loss of his touch between her legs. Her arse bumped against his crotch, and she began to rub herself against him. He clamped a hand upon her buttock to stop her.

He looked down at her smooth and unblemished rump. He had not paid much heed to this part of a woman's body before. Most that he had seen were flat or scrawny. But Miss Primrose had a derrière that commanded attention. It begged to be spanked.

"What is it you require of your submissive ones when you give them a hiding?" he asked, running his hand up and down the contour of the arse cheek.

"Your lordship?" she said, sounding a little dazed from her arousal.

"Do you make them count? Require they thank you? Demand they beg for more?"

She stiffened.

"Let's try all three," he said.

He slapped her bottom and waited. She started and said nothing.

"Miss Primrose?" he prompted.

"One."

Satisfied with the displeasure in her tone, he pressed, "And?"

Though he could not see her face, he would have bet she had rolled her eyes.

"Thank you…your lordship."

"I think we can do better. Let's try this once more."

He spanked her harder. She yelped. He waited.

"One. Thank you, your lordship."

"Much better. But you forgot to beg for more."

She made a growling sound. Delighted, he moved his hand and threaded his fingers through the hairs at the base of her pelvis. He could smell her arousal, and it made his blood pound.

"Come, you are no dunce, Miss Primrose. You will do this correctly."

He smacked the other cheek. The delicious half-sphere quivered briefly.

"One! Thank you, your lordship! Please, spank me again!"

"Perfection."

If she could see him, he imagined she would be glaring daggers at him. He gently caressed her rump before landing another whack. This time she cried out.

"Two! Thank you, your lordship. Please, spank me…again."

"Happy to oblige."

He walloped the same cheek. She cried out once more. Her derrière blushed from the attention. It deserved to be covered in welts, the same ones Mr. Fields described Nicholas and William to possess. But, gazing at her rump, Spencer could not bring himself to mar such lovely flesh—yet.

"Three. Thank you, your lordship. Please, spank me again."

"Well done, Miss Primrose."

His compliment was received without welcome. She simply snorted in response. Bringing his arm up, he brought his hand against her with greater force. She choked on her breath. Her hands clenched into her bindings.

"Four," she said when her breath returned. "Thank you, your lordship. Please...spank me again."

"As you wish."

He dealt her a lighter blow.

"Six. Th—Seven! Eight!" She gasped for breath. "Thank you, your l-lordship. Please spank me again."

He felt a rush. Perhaps he was capable of more cruelty than he thought. If only Nicholas could share in his satisfaction.

"How many do you think you can sustain, Miss Primrose?"

She shook her head.

"How high have you gone? How many strikes have you imparted upon a man's arse?"

"I don't remember. Nine! Thank you, your lordship. Please spank me again. A dozen, perhaps? Ten!"

"Try fifty. The most I have ever seen landed upon a man was thirty. And we are at but ten."

She groaned and strained against his neckcloth. He stared at her arse. His cock was hard as stone. He imagined it going in and out of that luscious rump of hers. His next thwack sent her to her toes.

"Eleven...Thank you, your lordship...Please spank me again." Her voice trembled.

"But...we have time," he said, taking a step back. "I promise you that we will have achieved fifty, perhaps more, before the sennight is done."

*****

Beatrice suppressed an oath. Eyes shut, she forced herself to take a calming breath. Her arse smarted something fierce. To make matters worse, she could feel the wetness of her arousal sliding down her thigh. She could not survive fifty such wallops as he had delivered. Surely he could not mean what he had said? But her fear was displaced when he began stroking her between the legs. The pleasure, coupled with the pain, formed an exquisite pairing, like purposeful discordancy in a musical composition, or a sorbet on a summer day. As a dominant one, she more readily understood the erotic effect of power over another, but she had a newfound appreciation for the role of a submissive.

An *inkling* of appreciation, she allowed. She had known it to be futile, even detrimental, to protest or defy him. She owned her error and possessed too much integrity to eschew blame, but she had not enjoyed having to thank him and ask to be spanked when she wanted none of it. She hoped he was done with the punishment. She had let slip two little words, yet from his reaction, one would think she had cursed his mother with the worst obscenities. What the devil was so offensive in the words *my pet*? The man was beyond her comprehension.

But he had the most delectable hands, and a touch that made her legs weaken. His middle finger entered her quim now, taking his time exploring her most private orifice, finding a spot that sent shivers to the tips of her digits. He withdrew, dragging the finger along her clitoris. The pain of his spanking magnified the beauty of his caresses. Perhaps he would reward her for having taken the punishment without complaint. Her cunnie grasped at his finger as he pushed it back into her, gradually coaxing her back to that desirable agitation. She angled her hips, that he could push his finger deeper into her. As if reading her mind, he pressed two fingers into her and quickened his motions, rubbing a sensitive area in the front of her cunnie. Her orgasm loomed. She groaned. He slowed.

He repeated this pattern several times, bringing her excitement to a boil, then retreating till she returned to a simmer. When he had done this dance with her for the third time, she realized he did not mean to reward her. Instead, her body reached a level of distress that made the spanking preferable. She began cursing him in her head.

"You mean to be cruel, your lordship," she said, omitting words that related to the anus of a donkey.

"You wish to spend."

"May I, your lordship?" It took some effort to speak the words without sarcasm. "Please, your lordship."

He stroked her harder and faster. The summit came into view once more. Wonderful sensations fanned from deep within her. She could feel them coming to a peak. Yes, yes…she could almost forgive him his impertinence if he led her to spend.

"No…" she gasped when he withdrew from her completely.

He tweaked her clitoris. She could not see him, but she heard him walk to some other part of the room and open a drawer. No, a trunk.

"I had your artifacts brought to me from the Inn," he said. "Including a rather large cage of sorts, which now sits in the stables. My butler wondered if I meant to add a new mastiff to my kennel."

Her eyes grew wide. She had but used the cage once, upon

Nicholas. She had found the contraption revulsive, but Nicholas, she had reasoned, was no better than a dog. Nicholas had not complained, but she would not suffer being put in a cage. Not even for a hundred quid.

"Do you have a fetish for nipples, Miss Primrose?" he asked, standing behind the footboard so that she could see him. He held two small clamps linked together by a small chain. "You will be satisfied to know that mine are still raw from your attentions last night. Yours, however, will be more sore."

He fixed one onto her nipple. She sucked in her breath at the pinching pain. He wrapped the chain around the bedpost and affixed the other clamp. She now fully understood why Nicholas and William howled when she had applied the clamps to them. But she would not give *his lordship* the satisfaction of her cries.

"Do you still wish to spend?"

She closed her eyes so as not to glare at him. She focused on the rhythm of her breathing.

"Do you, Miss Primrose?"

"If you wish it, your lordship."

"You may avail yourself of the bedpost."

She stared at him. He wished her to rut against the bedpost like a beast in heat?

"Come, you are free to be the vulgar, lascivious strumpet that you are."

He tugged the chain, and she cried out at the tension upon her nipples. Propping a knee upon the bed, she opened her thighs and attempted to angle herself against the wooden post. She hesitated at the awkwardness, wondering if it would be better if she draped the leg over the footboard. He pulled on the chain to urge her along. She managed to fit her cunnie against the post.

Grabbing the post with her hands for support, she did her

best to slide herself along it. At first she knew only discomfort, but when she found a tolerable position, the pleasure returned. Letting go her last shred of shame and decency, she ground herself against the bedpost. On occasion he would pull upon the chain, but the ache in her nipples sent jolts to her cunnie, increasing her desire to spend. She would not have thought it possible, being tied to a bedpost, having endured a sound spanking, her nipples in pinched torment, that she could be sufficiently aroused. It was not easy, but the end was in sight.

"Enough," he said hoarsely. The pupils of his eyes had melted, and lust was etched in his features. Releasing the chain, he went to stand behind her.

Fuck me, please, she pleaded silently. She heard him rustle with his clothing. He pulled her leg off the bed and gripped her hips with both hands. She felt the head of his erection against her arse. He pulled her onto her toes and guided his cock beneath her and into her soaking cunnie. *Glory*!

He groaned as her cunnie grabbed at him greedily. "You'll not treat the bedpost better than you would a real cock?"

Arching her arse, though it was no easy feat with the bedpost digging into her bosom, she attempted to hump his shaft. Being on her toes gave her little leverage, but after several tries, he assisted her with his own thrusts. His pelvis smacked against her, and she could feel the hairs there upon her bottom. The bedpost pressed against her harder every time he drove into her, but she did not care. That divine release approached and soon threw her under its spasmodic currents. She disintegrated into nerves convulsing between the hardness of his body and the rigidity of the bedpost. She knew she screamed, but the voice came from another place—the rafters, perhaps. He thrust into her in rapid succession to bring on his own release. He spent, jerking against her violently, just before she collapsed and slid to her knees. Stumbling, he fell onto the bed.

Somewhere outside a wren sang, but the sound could only be heard between the intervals of their panting. When he had caught his breath, he untied the sheath from his cock and replaced his fall for the third time that morning. He then removed her bindings and the clamps upon her nipples. He caught her before she crumpled to the floor and lay her upon the bed. She was sore all over.

"Well done, my pet," he said.

Beatrice silently cursed. The tables had turned…for good.

PART V

Punishing Miss Primrose

Punishing Miss Primrose, Part V

THE MARQUESS OF CAREY wondered that he would ever be able to fuck again after his sennight with Miss Beatrice Primrose concluded. He had already spent thrice within one morning—and after a most haggard night in which his orgasm had been stalled by a most vicious ointment. He found gratification in having had his way with Miss Primrose partially on behalf of his younger brother, Nicholas, who, from the reports Mr. Fields had provided, was not granted access to her body. A work of sin was Miss Primrose, her body speaking more temptations than the serpent of Eden.

Miss Primrose covered herself with a banyan, and he was glad not to have the distracting sight of her naked body. With knit brows, she eyed the chamber pot he had set aside earlier. She looked at him and her frown deepened.

"Do you still insist on playing the part of my maid?" she asked, her tone a touch less arch than before.

"There is a commode in the closet beside the bathing tub," he relented, hiding a smile at his own mischievousness at not having told her of the commode the first time she voiced her need to attend nature's call. Instead, he had led her to believe that she would have to perform the act before him.

Realizing his previous purposeful omission, she narrowed her eyes at him, and he thought if she had the chance to kill him, or at least maim him, she'd have done so. But she was clearly also relieved to have the opportunity for privacy and departed with quick steps. When she had closed the door behind her, Spencer ran his thumb along his jaw. If she displeased him greatly, he might not offer the use of the commode next time. She deserved none of the niceties he had shown her. She deserved to rot in one of those cages they used at that den of sin and lechery dubbed the Inn of the Red Chrysanthemum. Instead, he had allowed her to dine at his table yester evening, provided her with one of the nicer guest chambers, and allowed her to spend when she deserved no such pleasure after what she had done to his brother, Nicholas, and cousin, William.

He walked over to the one window with its curtains still drawn. He had dismissed all the servants this morning so that they would not bear witness to her "screams ringing from the rafters," leaving Miss Primrose sans the abigail she had brought with her and no one to interfere with his plans. There was no place for Miss Primrose to flee. Even if she knew the location of his estate, they were miles from anyone and a good day's travel to London. He had been rather fortunate that she had accepted his proposition without a great deal of questions, but he had offered her a sum of money she could not refuse—a sum the grasping harlot had demanded be doubled.

After opening the curtains to reveal the grey summer morning, the paper upon the writing table nearby caught his eye. Miss Primrose had glanced in its direction several times this morning. Wondering if it might have been left by a previous occupant of the chamber, however, he walked over to the table and picked up the sheet of paper. It was a letter addressed to "My

Dearest Niece." Hearing footsteps behind him, he turned to find Miss Primrose. She grabbed the letter from him.

"This is a private letter," she snapped.

"Your pardon," he replied. He had not seen much, only the salutation and the words *James took ill*. He had heard her mention a man by that name and assumed he was a lover, or at least an accomplice in her crimes.

She shoved the letter into a drawer and closed it tight. "I've no need for your help, but you are welcome to watch me dress."

He watched her retrieve her clothes for the second time. How was it she could find a way to assert herself, granting him audience as if she were in control, when he had made it clear to her that he would have the dominant role and she the submissive counterpart? If his presence discomfited her while she dressed, she showed no evidence of it this time. She had not enjoyed stepping out of the bath while he held the towel, but perhaps she had acclimated to being disrobed before him, especially after he had tied her, naked, to the bedpost and fucked her.

His blood warmed at the memory of his cock sliding beneath her arse, her supple derrière ramming into his pelvis. He shook his head, amazed that he could desire her so. Her hair was far too curly for his tastes, and he had not thought he could find her darker coloring becoming. But he had been quickly disavowed of his old notions of beauty, and despite—or because of—his deep antipathy toward her, his appetite for her had grown. "She makes hungry where most she satisfies," Shakespeare had written of the Queen of Egypt. Miss Primrose made a fitting Cleopatra. Poor Nicholas might have become her doomed Mark Antony had Spencer not discovered them. From Mr. Fields, a Bow Street Runner he had hired to follow Nicholas, he had a grim and shocking account of what Miss Primrose had done to his brother as well as to William.

When he was done with Miss Primrose, Spencer determined, Cleopatra would be no more, a threat to men no longer. He would emerge the victor. Like Octavius Caesar.

But first you must resist her charms, warned his intellect. He admitted it was no easy feat. He better understood why Nicholas had written in his letter, begging her to take him back as her lover, that he could not live without her. William was not as devastated as Nicholas at having been cast off by her, but he owned he would not have hesitated to return to her if asked. The admission had prompted Spencer to send the two young men off to Belgium while he dealt with the temptress, a wanton whore who worked at Madame Devereux's Inn of the Red Chrysanthemum. Like a witch, Miss Primrose had an uncanny ability to cast a spell upon men. If not for his desire to provide her a set-down, to punish her for her dastardly treatment of Nicholas and William, he, too, might have succumbed to her. That recognition, and apprehension, of his own susceptibility fueled his anger toward her.

But the anger also seemed to encourage his lust. Even now, as he watched her slip into her shift and lace her short stays, he could not help but admire the swell of her hips; her large brown areolas, briefly exposed; and that ample hoydenish arse. How delectable that flesh had felt against his hand, quivering after each slap, its cheeks burning red from the spanking. Without invitation, remembering that she had pricked herself before, he went to assist her with the pins to her gown. She did not object and tolerated the extra effort he required to manipulate the tiny pins with his masculine fingers.

Struck once more by the plainness and thinness of her

garments, he had an epiphany. "This fellow James takes the gains of your *activities*."

She tensed, and her breath stopped.

"Will he not allow you to procure better attire?" he continued. "It would seem a wise investment."

She exhaled. "He is not my go-between."

"Clearly, Madame Devereux is your bawd. But what has he done to merit a share of your earnings?"

Turning, she narrowed her eyes at him before walking over to the vanity and reaching for her hairbrush.

"I assume he must be your lover."

"La! Jealous are we?"

"Jealous?" he half-croaked, half-laughed. "I should want to be with a thieving strumpet?"

She glared at his reflection in the mirror. "I've not stolen a thing but a biscuit from my aunt's kitchen when I was a girl."

"You relieve men of their money through entrapment. There is little difference between you and a crook."

Her chin lifted. "You deem me a devious jezebel, but what does it say of your character when you desire me more than you would the most upright young woman of your precious *ton*."

His jaw tightened. "I own you are like a succulent cut of *beefsteak* to the gout: enticing to the beholder but perilous to one's health."

"Then your constitution must be extremely weak, for you have offered two hundred quid to partake of beefsteak for an entire sennight."

He folded his arms. "I am not afflicted with the gout."

She finished brushing her hair and wrapped it with a bandeau, then rose and said as she approached him, "I think, when we have done with the sennight, you will prefer the gout. Your desire for me will not be quenched in seven days time. It will have grown, and you will yearn—nay, burn—for more. And it will cost you more than two hundred quid for another taste. Unlike *beefsteak*."

His nostrils flared. She mocked his simile, but what disturbed him was the possible truth of her prophecy. Heat simmered in his loins. He would have thought his cock required a few hours respite, if not the entire day, after enduring the events of the morning. To ensure himself a reprieve, he would have to send Miss Primrose away.

"And if I am prone to surrendering to base, unhealthy urges, is it wise of you to provoke me?" he returned and had the satisfaction of seeing her retreat a step from him. He allowed she was no fool.

"You are free to wander about in any area save for the east wing," he said as he went to clear her breakfast tray. "I will summon you later."

She stiffened at the word *summon* but took his recommendation and departed the chambers. When she had gone, he let out a breath of relief. He took the tray down to the scullery. Having served as a sailor aboard a ship of the Royal Navy, he was no stranger to tasks beneath most men of his station. And he relished the momentary distraction from Miss Primrose. Later he would conduct a full inventory of the items in the trunk from the Red Chrysanthemum. The clamps he had affixed to her nipples had been delightful. He was sure the other baubles would prove equally devilish.

*****

Insufferable man, Beatrice huffed to herself. Perhaps it was she who ought to prefer the gout over the affliction, one that she shared with the nameless nobleman. She had few kind words for him, yet her body would respond to his caresses, would yearn to spend at his hand. She recalled the force with which he had smacked her derrière, but the walloping had only enflamed her lust further. She shivered to think that he might apply his hand to her backside *fifty* times instead of the eleven she had endured.

Wanting air, she looked and found a door to a veranda overlooking the gardens. She stepped outside and admired the view. A fountain stood near the entry of the garden. A half dozen wrens splashed in its pool. Perhaps later she would venture into the gardens to enjoy the summer flora. She knew not what *his lordship* intended, and the uncertainty unnerved her. But she had decided to see the sennight through. Six days remained. At their conclusion, she would have the remaining hundred quid he had promised. She would leave behind the whoring and return to Liverpool, to her aunt and nephew, James. She had not seen the boy for over a year and knew he must have grown dramatically in that time. She wondered if he would become a near replica of Nicholas Edelton.

While at the Inn of the Red Chrysanthemum, she had avenged her sister—and in some manner, James as well, for he would not have been born into the world and lost a mother if not for the treachery of William and Nicholas Edelton—and secured enough money to support her aunt and nephew for some time. As a bastard child, James would not have the privileges of his father, but Beatrice was determined that he should not want for much. She would put aside savings for his schooling when he came of age. She dreaded the day James would become old enough to inquire about his heritage. She had no answer yet for what she would say if he asked about his father.

Nicholas knew nothing of the child that had resulted from his rape of Charlotte. Though William was every bit as guilty as Nicholas in the evil deed, it was apparent that James, despite his youth, resembled Nicholas, whose slim figure and boyish physiognomy shared little with his cousin. William was tall with square shoulders and the same light brown hair as *his lordship*. She knew not which of the Edelton men had initiated the rape. Charlotte could only describe two drunken men assaulting her. But for Beatrice, both were culpable. Both were conceited young men of wealth and privilege, able to evade justice because of their standing. Both deserved the severest of punishments.

She wondered what had become of them. Though she could have continued her vengeance, humiliating them and flogging them to her heart's content, the efforts had wearied her over time. Nicholas had become smitten with her, catered to her every demand, offered her more than she had ever hoped to exact from him. After she had dismissed both men, Nicholas had written letters to her, beseeching his mistress to take him back. He persisted in returning to the Red Chrysanthemum till Madame Devereux declared him a nuisance and revoked his admission. Beatrice might have extended her stay at the Red Chrysanthemum, but she had no desire to ever cross paths with Nicholas or William again.

Finding a chair, she sat down and breathed in the country air. It smelled and tasted crisp compared to the city. She wondered at the distance to the nearest neighbor. In truth, she was a captive here, for while *his lordship* had said she could leave his estate at her will, he had not offered her any conveyance back to London. She hoped he would be civil enough to point her in the right direction. She had glimpsed indications of his decency, but he was too enigmatic for her to be certain. And she would have bet money that he disliked her in some form. Perhaps, upset that he was attracted to a dark whore, he directed his self-loathing toward her.

She did not like the situation. Accustomed to being in control, to issuing the commands, to hearing herself addressed as "Mistress Primrose," the role of the submissive one unsettled her. She was to address him as "his lordship," obey his directives, and be punished if he found her insubordinate. Thus far, she had committed one error. The penalty had not been too difficult to bear. Her arse had smarted beneath his hand, but the ache had faded faster than expected. The small metal clips he had affixed to her nipples produced a tolerable pain save when he pulled upon the chain between them. To her surprise, the sensations only added to her ardor.

Her stomach rumbled, and she wished she had taken his advice and eaten more of her breakfast. She considered going in search of the pantry when she heard footsteps behind her.

"I've prepared a light repast," his lordship said, approaching and setting down a tray with slices of meat, cheese, and bread upon the table beside her. "And this time, I require you to eat."

Without objection, she accepted the glass of lemonade he held out to her.

"The sweetmeats came from the gardens," he told her. "And you left this in the library."

She looked down at the tray and saw the book, *The Fortunes and Misfortunes of the Famous Moll Flanders*, she had pulled from the shelves yesterday. Remembering his comparison of her to the heroine of Defoe's novel, Beatrice said nothing. She reached for the bread and meat, making a sandwich, and took a hungry bite. He took the seat on the other side of the table and looked out over the gardens. He appeared more relaxed, and when the slight breeze tousled his hair, she was reminded of her previous hopes to have an enjoyable romp with the handsome stranger.

"You've no need to keep me company," she said. "I do perfectly well on my own."

"I have no intentions of a *tête-à-tête* but am here to ensure that you do not starve yourself."

"How gracious of your lordship."

He did not respond to her mockery. She swallowed the food in her mouth and, glancing at the book, wondered if a nicer disposition might gain her more. Though he insisted on having the dominant role, he had performed the duties of a servant, twice bringing her meals and drawing a bath for her.

"Thank you for the book," she tried.

A little startled, he replied, "You're welcome."

"You have a great many books in your library."

"My mother liked to read, and her tastes were diverse. From Shakespeare sonnets to original editions of French works. You are welcome to them."

"Thank you. I've not read but a handful of sonnets in my life. My French is too poor to attempt its literature."

He looked at her, curious. "You had a French tutor?"

"For but a year, and I fear my sister and I were poor students at the time. We ought to have made more of the brief opportunity."

"You have fallen far from grace. With your upbringing, you could have aspired to be a courtesan or become a mistress to a man of means or…"

"A man such as yourself?" she teased.

He frowned. "Your circumstances must have been drastic for you to end up in a brothel with Madame Devereux."

"My whoring," she went on, "is only temporary. I had…other motives for choosing the Red Chrysanthemum, which is not a brothel, though Madame is not averse to playing the bawd on occasion. The Inn is a club, of sorts, a place where its members can indulge in their most erotic penchants."

His eyes narrowed. "Is that all?"

"Its members seek and want to be there." Seeing the grim set of his features, she changed the subject. "But I have hopes that you will be my last patron. I shall seek employment hereafter as a governess or a lady's companion."

"You? A governess? You think you will be allowed the care of children?"

Offended by his skepticism, she replied, "I was a governess, beloved by the family, until…until I had to leave."

"It was discovered your virtue was lacking."

She scowled. "Yes, I had fucked the stable boy, the butler, the footman, my employer's valet, and I would have done the horses in the stable if I had stayed."

She nearly laughed at his open-mouthed stare.

"Which one of the fellows was James?"

Her cheeks burned. "None! I left because my sister fell ill."

He cleared his throat. "And you nursed her back to health."

Her bosom swelled. She could not respond, muted by the pain of her sister's death, which flared like a new wound, though she thought time and her vengeance upon Nicholas and William would have eased the loss. But this insolent nobleman, who presumed to know her and her situation, who assumed the worst of her because she was beneath his station in life, had somehow renewed the anguish and the misery. He suddenly represented all that she detested in Nicholas and William and men of their ilk.

"What do you care for the sister of a hedge-whore?" she replied and tossed the rest of her sandwich onto the tray.

He stared at the half-eaten sandwich. "You should finish it."

"*You* finish it if you care so much for it," she replied as she rose from her chair, too angry to form a mature response.

"At least eat the sweetmeats."

She would have, for she adored berries and did not often have them. But she wanted nothing of his at the moment.

"No, thank you," she replied and made for the stairs that led down to the gardens.

"You'll not have a chance to eat again till it is time for tea."

She ignored him and proceeded down the steps, needing to put some distance between them. For some strange reason, she felt as if she were looking at Nicholas and William when she saw him. But for his kind, she would still have a sister, her only sister.

She heard his footsteps behind her, and he grabbed her by the arm before she had reached the bottom of the stairs.

"You will eat more," he said when she faced him.

"I'm not hungry."

"I don't care."

Perhaps the painful memory, the knowledge of the crime that had been done to her sister pressed upon her mind too strongly at the moment, clouding her perception, but she felt as if she were staring at William Edelton.

"I'll not have the sweetmeats left on the tray," he said.

"Then shove them up your arse."

She attempted to wrench herself free, but he tightened his grip. Warning bells went off in her head, but before she could correct her impudence, he had lifted her and thrown her over his shoulder. He walked up the stairs back to the veranda, set her down, and bent her over the stone railing. The hard flat surface pressed into her ribcage and the lower half of her bosom.

"You'll want the sweetmeats now, I warrant," he said, then flipped her skirts over her hips, baring her bottom.

Thank God the servants were away! she thought to herself. His hand pressed upon her back, keeping her against the railing.

"But there is a lesson to be learned here," he continued. "It is much wiser to heed me without the opposition."

He smacked a cheek with his free hand.

"Now, Miss Primrose, we will finish the sweetmeats. Do you understand?"

She was to receive another spanking, she realized. A part of her did not want to give in. The other part warned her that she had no choice. She had survived the one from this morning. How much more did he intend?

He whacked her again, but this time she howled. Something harder and unyielding had struck her. She realized he had picked up *Moll Flanders.*

"Are we agreed, Miss Primrose?"

"Y-yes."

She grasped the railing, attempting to alleviate the pressure of being ground into the stone. He held a berry before her. She opened her mouth and accepted the fruit. When she was done chewing, he walloped her again with the book. She cursed aloud.

"But I—" she began.

"Fail to eat and I'll double the blows," he explained, offering her another berry.

She ate the second one and silently cursed him, then braced herself for another smack. She could hardly believe what was happening to her. Her arse was exposed to the world and she was compelled to take food from his hand as if she were a babe or a dog—all while receiving a paddling with a copy of Moll Flanders! A part of her wanted to cry. The other part vowed vengeance. She would procure her own sweetmeats and shove them up his anus—with a hard wooden spoon.

He struck her twice when she did not immediately take the third berry into her mouth. The air felt cool about her nakedness, but her arse burned. She ate the next one quickly and he seemed to ease the force of the subsequent blow. But the fifth one nearly sent her over the railing. She wanted to beg him to stop, though her pride would never allow such a thing. After the sixth application, he paused. She hoped the last of the sweetmeats had gone. His hand slid between her thighs. He withdrew it, wet.

No! How was this possible? Perhaps the current hiding reminded her of the delectable fucking that had followed the spanking from the morning? Did her body now interpret pain as pleasure?

He inserted a finger between her folds. She shivered. His breathing had become uneven. Would he take her again? She rather hoped he would. He seemed to contemplate the possibility. But it was unlikely he had brought a sheath with him. And given how forcefully he could thrust, a pounding against the rough railing might not prove that pleasant.

"What is the lesson we have learned, Miss Primrose?" he asked.

She groaned at the patronization but answered, "To heed your lordship."

"Heed and obey."

Since he could not see her face, she rolled her eyes. Her buttocks ached twice as bad as before.

Without replacing her skirts, he threw her once more over his shoulder, making sure to grab the book before he entered the house.

*****

Why did she not eat the damn sweetmeats? Spencer wondered as he tossed her onto her bed. Not that he did not enjoy bending her over the railing and palming that delicious arse once more. It took all of him not to take her then and there. But he had none of her condoms upon him. And he was not finished with her punishment.

He understood that he had provoked her and made unkind remarks. While his assumptions may not have been on the mark, he was not far off the truth. It was her place to submit to his accusations. That she did not, taking offense and mocking him instead, irritated him. He recognized that the subject of her sister was a tender one, but he was too enflamed at present over her suggestion regarding the sweetmeats to dwell on the matter. He could not remember the last time someone had spoken to him with such insolence.

"What are you doing?" she asked as she watched him open the trunk of items from the Red Chrysanthemum.

"What is this?" He held up an iron bar with cuffs at both ends of it. Mr. Fields had not described this particular article in his reports.

She said nothing.

"Are we dismayed? I assure you I intend to try every one of these intriguing implements before our time here is done. Now, what is this?"

"A spreading bar," she muttered.

He walked over to her with it in hand. "Show me how it works."

Her countenance tightened, but she took the bar from his hands. "The cuffs go about the ankles. The bar prevents the legs from closing."

"Demonstrate."

With tentative hands, she locked the cuffs about her ankles. His cock, already hard, throbbed against his trousers.

"Now undress."

"Again?!"

"Worry not. You will not be required to don your garments again."

Her eyes widened.

"You should try to be a more apt pupil, Miss Primrose."

"I erred," she said after some struggle. "Your comments had incensed me, but I ought not have told you to shove the sweetmeats…"

"Up my arse."

"I won't make the same mistake."

"Is it not common practice at the Red Chrysanthemum for the submissive ones to forego clothing?"

"Sometimes."

"Do you allow your *pets* clothing?"

She frowned.

"I thought not."

He found the pincushion and handed it to her. The heat was going to his head, but he could not stop. The more she defied him, the more demanding he wanted to be.

After removing the pins, she removed her gown with some difficulty as she was sitting on the bed with the spreading bar between her legs. He made no move to help her and watched as she untied her petticoats. She had to lift her derrière to push them down her legs. He adjusted the tenting at his crotch, wondering how long he could refuse his cock satisfaction. Next she unlaced her stays. After her stays, she pulled her arms from her shift and slowly pushed it down past her breasts. His cock reared its head at the sight of her two magnificent orbs. With the shift removed, she sat upon the bed naked but for her stockings, garters, and the spreading bar. Her body was an amazing sight to behold for she was near hairless compared to women of paler skin. Walking over, he brushed his hand along her leg. Her limbs were uncommonly smooth. His lust swelled.

"I did as you bid, my lord," she said.

"Yes," he acknowledge hoarsely as his gaze devoured her. "You are learning. Finally."

Remembering he had found her wet after the spanking downstairs, he said, "Pleasure yourself."

"Yes, my lord."

She fitted her hand between her thighs and began to play with the little bud at the top of her folds. He rubbed his cock through his fall. He sensed her awkwardness but wondered if she were aroused enough that she would spend before him. How long would it take to make herself spend?

"Lie back," he said, wanting a fuller view of her cunnie.

The moisture there allowed her fingers to slide along her slit more quickly. He walked around to the other side of the bed for a view of her tits. In the undulations and planes of her body from her groin to her belly to her breasts he found not the slightest flaw. Her head rested near the edge of the bed, and though he had intended to search for the condoms that she kept, he could not wait. He undid his fall and pulled out his cock. He caressed its length.

"Come closer," he said.

He rubbed his cock against her plump lips. Anticipating what he wanted, she opened her mouth and took him in. He groaned at the lushness enveloping his shaft. The angle of her throat as her head hung off the edge fit well with the angle of his cock, and he pushed himself deeper into her orifice. She gagged but quickly relaxed. She wrapped a hand about the base of his cock to ensure its position. With her other hand, she continued to fondle herself. He grabbed both breasts and mauled them, then tugged at her nipples and twisted them. Her hips came off the bed. She yelped, but the sounds were muffled by his cock. When she tried to disengage, he smacked the side of an orb. The sight of her body, of her pleasuring herself, and the feel of her mouth about his cock was too much. He began thrusting his hips at her face. She grabbed him with both hands to prevent him from penetrating her throat too deeply or striking her in a place that made her choke. He replaced the hand between her legs with his own. The more she writhed, the harder he rubbed.

"Oh, God," he groaned as the pressure mounted in his groin.

He pumped himself into her, and the tension soon shot through his cock, spilling into her cavity. She started to gag. He pulled out to relieve her choking, a string of his semen falling upon her cheek. His body jerked and shuddered. After shaking off the violence of his orgasm, he resumed fondling her. With his other hand, he kneaded her breast and flicked the nipple with his thumb. She grabbed the bed linen beneath her, perhaps to keep from sliding off the edge of the bed, but she was nearing her own climax.

Seeing the crest of the wave, he intensified his touch until she cried out, her body shaking and thrashing upon the bed. Her wetness streamed from her, startling him and coating his fingers with her fluid. He eased his caresses. Her cries became groans. He lifted her and placed her more fully upon the bed. Her breathing was heavy, and his seed glistened upon her lips and cheek. He fell onto the bed beside her. Before drifting into sleep, he wondered if he might not end up more like Mark Antony than Octavius Caesar.

*****

When Beatrice opened her eyes, she noted the afternoon sunlight beaming through the window. Lifting her head, she saw *his lordship* sitting in the same chair they had fucked in earlier that day. A light blanket covered her, and the spreading bar was no longer affixed to her ankles. She looked next for the garments she had taken off, but they were nowhere to be found.

"There is a tray of tea upon the table in the anteroom," he told her.

She raised her brows. "You made tea?"

"It is not that difficult."

What a peculiar man he was, she thought to herself as she pulled the blanket tighter about her. Despite having been *au naturel* before him several times now, she did not like the exposure. Perhaps because she did not want to give him the satisfaction of viewing her body. Or perhaps because her nakedness symbolized her subordinate position *vis-à-vis* his.

"Where are my clothes?" she asked.

"You won't need them."

With dread, she realized he meant what he had said earlier. He held up a silver chain linked to two more chains. A small clamp dangled from each end.

"You may retain your garters and stockings," he said, "but this is all you may wear."

She sucked in her breath. "And this is to atone for what transgression?"

His jaw hardened. "None in particular."

She lifted her chin. He wanted to assert his domination, did he?

Standing, he placed the chain upon the sideboard. "Dinner will be ready at six o'clock. You may bring the tea tray down at that time. I shall have fires burning in the library and the drawing room. At no time shall I find you have donned any other article of clothing. Do you understand, Miss Primrose?"

"Yesss."

"Good."

Without further word, he turned and left. With a cry of aggravation, she fell back into the bed. Perhaps she could stay in her chambers the rest of the day. She saw that *Moll Flanders* lay upon the bedside table. Grabbing the book, she opened it. But after reading the first few sentences, she lost focus. Pondering the strangeness of her situation had not provided any enlightenment thus far, but she could not resist ruminating. Perhaps she should simply acquiesce to all of his demands, as the submissive patrons at the Red Chrysanthemum did, without complaint or resistance. However, she had the suspicion that even unwavering submission would not please him enough. She was sure she could play the part of a submissive one with more obedience than she had, if only *his lordship* did not vex her so much.

Feeling hungry, she hopped out of bed and went into the anteroom to partake of the tea and edibles he had provided. She then spent the rest of the afternoon contemplating the best course of action with his lordship, reading the first chapter of *Moll Flanders*, and drafting a letter to her aunt. She wrote to Sophie that she hoped to be in Liverpool within two fortnights with over a hundred quid, which ought to sustain them quite well till she secured employment. She could hardly wait to see James and did not think she would miss much of London at all but that she would bring them both something, perhaps some lace or notions for Sophie and a toy for James.

The small clock above the fireplace chimed the hour, startling her. She saw that it was six o'clock. She doubted *his lordship* would approve of her tardiness. Quickly, she went to the sideboard and looked down at the thin three-pronged chain. He had made his expectations clear. She picked up the silver chain and clamped one end upon the base of the nipple. She knew that part to be less sensitive than the tip. She applied the second clamp to the other nipple. The pinching was bearable. She held the third clamp for some time before spreading her thighs and reaching for her clit. She grunted as she clipped the chain in place. It felt tighter than she would have liked. Her cunnie pulsed at the constant pressure near it.

Gingerly, she slipped on her shoes and carefully made her way out the bedchamber and down the stairs to the dining room as quickly as she could, though the faster she moved, the more she felt the clamps pulling upon her. She could feel the metal clamp upon her clit with every step. She tried walking with her thighs further apart so that they did not rub and brush against the clamp. The rest of her body might as well not have existed. The contrivance made her aware of only her nipples and clit.

He stood waiting for her beside the table. She found it difficult to meet his gaze at first, but she was curious to see his reaction. He seemed frozen by the sight of her. His stare could have cut through steel. Her mood improved. She had not lost all hope of domination. She fingered the chain that led between her thighs.

"I do not often wear jewelry," she said. "Does this one suit me?"

He said nothing but reached for the chain. His gaze went from the tiny links to her breasts. Lightly, he tugged upon the chain. She gasped at the increased tension upon her.

"It suits you well," he replied.

Dropping the chain, he pulled out a chair for her. She sat down and examined the covered bowl before her.

"Cook baked enough bread for several days," he said as he went to sit at the head of the table. "My culinary skills are limited, so you will have to settle for a simple rabbit stew."

He took the lid off his bowl, and she did the same. The stew looked and smelled decent enough. Hungry, she helped herself to the bread and glass of burgundy before her. They ate in silence for most of the meal. Still not comfortable dining in the nude, she was too cognizant of the clamps upon her private parts. There was, too, a sense of arousal.

"I have business to attend to in the morning," he said when he had finished. "You may have to mind your own toilette."

She perked at not having to wear the chain and clamps all day.

"You shall wear what I have placed upon the chair beside your chamber door."

She frowned but managed to reply, "Yes, my lord."

"Do you wish to have dessert?"

She shook her head.

"Then we are done for the evening. You are free to return to your chambers. If you wish to have a fire, I can start one for you."

"That won't be necessary. I think I shall retire for the evening."

She was unsure if she ought be disappointed that he was not aroused enough to take her. She had half expected him to throw her upon the dining table, but she was relieved, too, and took advantage of her dismissal and returned to her room. There she removed the clamps from her nipples and the one from her clitoris. She rubbed the soreness there. What a thing to be sitting at that table sans any clothing while *his lordship* dined as if nothing were amiss! She could barely taste the food, the majority of her focus being the damned clips upon the nubs of her body. Her fingers worked the poor little bud between her folds. The blood had rushed to the area when she removed the clamp. The flesh felt extremely sensitive…and stimulated.

Crawling into bed, she swirled her fingers about her clitoris, stoking the arousal. What a confounding mess she was! The paces he put her through were awkward, provoking, and even humiliating. His condescension and derogatory remarks infuriated her. Yet he managed, despite all this, to excite her. Was she mad? Had lust overtaken all her faculties? She quickened her strokes, recalling all that he had done to her and the paroxysms that he had led her to. She thought of how she had ridden his cock and if there might be another opportunity to do so. Would he allow her to apply any of the implements of pain-pleasure to him?

With a small cry, she brought herself to spend. The orgasm was minor compared to the ones she had experienced earlier. She wanted to spend at his hand and hoped to do so tomorrow. Nonetheless, she was relieved to hear that he would be gone in the morning, providing her a little respite from his vexing company. Her instincts told her he was no fool, no madman, nor lecher, nor wicked ogre, but his anger toward her was real. She was not satisfied that it stemmed merely from self-loathing.

Weary from the events of the last four and twenty hours, she began to drift to sleep, promising herself that she would do a full exploration of his lordship's residence tomorrow. She wanted to understand his strong and mysterious sentiments toward her. Above all, she tired of his namelessness. Perhaps the east wing, though he had forbidden her to go there, held the answers. While he was away on business in the morning, she would begin her investigation there.

She slept soundly and dreamless. Emerging from the deep

sleep some time later, however, she heard the crackle of the fireplace. Her eyes fluttered. The glow in her room confirmed the presence of fire. When the realization of this sank in, she pried her eyes open and found *his lordship* standing at the foot of her bed, holding a cord of rope with one end tied to the top of the bedpost. His countenance was somber and his tone mirthless when he spoke.

"I think it time I repaid your favor of last night, Miss Primrose."

###

PUNISHING MISS PRIMROSE, PARTS VI - X

PREORDER THE EBOOK FOR ONLY $0.99!!
LIMITED TIME ONLY*

ON SALE JULY 1, 2014
Regular EBOOK Price $3.29
PRINT PRICE TBD

Can't wait?

For a FREE copy of Punishing Miss Primrose, Part VI, sign up for the Erotic Historicals quarterly newsletter at www.EroticHistoricals.com

*Pre-orders are available at select retailers. For more information, visit www.EroticHistoricals.com.

Excerpt from
Submitting to the Rake

The Earl folded his arms and waited. His frown did not diminish.

"If there is a shred of decency in you," she began.

He lifted his brows. "I thought I was devoid of morals."

She winced, regretting her earlier words, but there was nothing to be done. She could not retract what she had said earlier, so she forged ahead.

"You have no need of someone like Josephine. Someone of your, well, stature can command any number of other women. Josephine is not worth your time."

"Rather harsh words for a cousin you adore."

"I meant…" she bristled.

"I know what you meant, Miss Merrill, but my mind has not changed on the matter since last we met, and I do not appreciate attempts to meddle in my affairs. I wonder that your cousin approves of it, but I take it she does not realize you are here?"

Again, she flushed. "I am here on her behalf, even if she does not approve of what I do. I realize I risk her affection, but I could not stand idly by and watch her demise. She may not know it, but she requires my aid."

"Noble if not condescending sentiments. Your cousin is a grown woman, not in leading strings."

"She is young and does not appreciate the arts a man of your sort would employ."

This time it was he who turned color. "A man of my sort?"

Would he have her explain all to him? Heloise wondered, feeling a dangerous pit opening up before her.

"I think you know to what I allude," she evaded.

"If by that you mean your shallow view of my association with women..."

Heloise blinked. *He* was the rake and would yet criticize *her* character? The man was beyond monstrous.

He continued, "...I quite understand people of *your* sort and how threatened you feel by my enlightened position on women."

"Enlightened? Is that how you defend your wanton ways?"

He clucked his tongue. "Tisk, tisk. You make it sound vulgar, Miss Merrill. Why scorn the innate urges, the natural passions of our bodies?"

Her heart began to pound once more. Something in the way he spoke, the rich tenor of his voice, the enunciation – as if he were caressing the words – made her skin warm.

"The rhetoric of one who lacks the resolve to resist the base desires..." she responded, but her tone lacked confidence even to her own ears.

He took a step towards her, and despite the lethargy she had felt from her journey and lack of sleep, every nerve in her body came to life.

"Are you possessed of such resolve, Miss Merrill?" he inquired.

His gaze seemed to probe into her past, and she was sure he saw it all.

"That is none of your concern and irrelevant to the matter at hand," she said quickly.

"You made it my concern when you chose to meddle in my affairs," he replied grimly, advancing another step.

"I think, I am not possessed of the same, er, passions as you," she answered, taking a step back.

"Indeed? How sad. Perhaps that can be changed."

"I have no wish to change."

"You may feel differently in a sennight hence."

A sennight hence? What did he mean by that? Instinctively, she glanced towards the door, her escape, but it was too far. And *he* stood in her path.

"I have no plans to keep my own company for the next three days," he elaborated. "And as you have deprived me of Miss Josephine, you will have to take her place."

"I have no intention of staying," she protested, trying to stave off the panic that gripped her heart. But it was not the fear of immediate harm that alarmed her. It was…the flush of excitement coursing in her own body, a sensation reminiscent of a time long ago when she did not ignore her curiosity or the urges of the flesh.

"Your intentions matter not. My coach will return you home only on my command."

"You mean to keep me here? Against my will?" she cried.

"You came of your own free will, Miss Merrill. I would have advised against it."

"I am to be your prisoner?" she attempted with what little indignation she could muster to mask her agitation.

He advanced towards her, but she stepped back until the back of her knees struck the bed. The nearness of his body took the air from her. The flush in her body grew.

"Do you know what I do with meddlers?" he asked.

Trapped between him and the bed behind her, all she could do was hold his gaze. Her mind grasped for a rejoinder but came up empty.

"I punish them, Miss Merrill."

Excerpt from
Mastering the
Marchioness

Hanging from a hook, her toes barely touched the floor. Instead of the mask worn by many of the other guests at Madame Botreaux's Cavern of Pleasures, the young woman wore only a silk red blindfold. The rest of her was laid bare for all to see.

Vale Montressor Aubrey, the third Marquess of Dunnesford, circled around her like a predator examining its prey, occasionally running the tip of a riding crop languidly over her nipples. Once or twice he pulled the riding crop back and flicked it against a breast. She gasped, then groaned.

"Please…please, Master…" she pleaded.

Peering at her thighs through his black and silver mask, Vale saw the telltale glisten of moisture at her mons. This one never took long.

"Your punishment has hardly begun, m'dear," Vale told her.

"Please…forgive me…I was weak."

Suppressing a sigh, Vale pulled back the crop and lashed it at her buttocks. It was unfortunate. Her body was beautiful – with full ripe breasts that quivered when punished – but she had indeed proven weak.

"I leave you to contemplate how you can do better," Vale said with another swat of the crop.

As he headed toward the stairs, past a number of men and women engaged in various forms of coupling, a masked woman threw herself at his feet.

"Take me – I would be a far better submissive than she," the woman declared.

Vale looked down at her. His half-mask did not cover his frown or the hard set of his jaw, and she crept away in shame.

"Pray tell that is not boredom writ on your face?" asked Lance Duport when Vale joined his friend and Madame Botreaux in the balcony from where they could view the activity below, much like patrons in an opera box.

It was the favorite spot of Penelope Botreaux. She rarely ventured onto the floor of the Cavern of Pleasures – so-called because the largeassembly area existed practically in the basement of her residence. Unfinished walls left the ground rock exposed. As there were no windows, only the dim glow of a few strategically placed candelabras penetrated the darkness.

"I let you have the beauty when I could have made her mine," Penelope declared from the settee upon which she lounged like a Grecian goddess, wearing a thin transparent gown over a body that time and a few too many glasses of ratafia had made plump in various places.

"I regret your generosity is wasted on me," Vale replied, removing his mask and looking over the balcony to where he had left the young woman. "Perhaps I am too old for her."

Penelope snorted. "I am over forty and hardly consider myself old. You are barely five and thirty."

"And you could best any of the younger men here," added Lance as he raked an appreciative gaze over Vale's body.

An active life of riding, hunting, fencing, and an occasional bout in the ring kept Vale's physique in admirable shape. His stockings encased calves that were the envy of his peers. His simple linen shirt opened to reveal a broad, strong chest. His tight breeches covered muscular thighs and left little to the imagination.

Lance turned to Penelope. "You know half the women here – and men – would give their right buttock to be partnered with Vale. He needs more than a neophyte."

"Would *you* give your right buttock?" Penelope returned.

Lance curled his thin lips into a salacious grin. "I would give both my buttocks. Do you remember Demarco?"

"Ah, yes, how can I not? He was a great but beautiful brute. A Samson with that lush head of hair."

"And cocky as hell, but Vale had him writhing in submission within the hour. After such a conquest, I wonder that Vale should wish to trifle with the weaker sex."

Vale smiled. "Despite all appearances, women are not the weaker sex."

"Well, what the devil are you looking for?" Penelope prodded. "Apparently not men, nor women of unsurpassed beauty. You have spurned both novice and skilled submissives. Only Lovell Elroy has had more partners than you."

Vale pressed his lips into a grim line as he looked over the balcony at a man wearing a red mask flogging a woman. "Lovell is malicious. He cares nothing for the women he is with. I wish you would throw him out, Penelope."

"But the women flock to him – especially those whose hearts you have broken."

"Lovell breaks more than hearts, Penelope."

"Ah well, like you, he is a beautiful specimen to behold, and I do enjoy beauty." Penelope held up her quizzing glass and blatantly directed her gaze at Vale's crotch.

"Egad, Vale," Lance interjected. "Nearly forgot: felicitations to you on your recent nuptials."

Vale started. He had nearly forgotten that he was now married.

"Indeed," Penelope said. "Where are you hiding this wife of yours?"

"We arrived in town but yesterday," Vale answered. "She is with my cousin Charlotte at the moment."

He was not particularly interested in pursuing the subject. Though he was sure that Charlotte would prove better company for Harrietta than he, he nonetheless felt a stab of guilt for pawning his wife off on a relative for the evening.

"And will you be introducing us to her?"

"Good God, no," Vale shot back. "She is a simple girl from the country."

"Hardly sounds like the sort of woman you would choose to marry after all these years," Lance commented.

Vale shrugged. "Dunnesford needs an heir. Does it matter whom I marry?"

"Yes, but of all the beautiful and wealthy women setting their caps at you, why a chit for whom you seem to have ambivalent feelings?"

"Her brother and I were the best of friends before he died at Yorktown in the service of His Majesty. We served in the same regiment for some time together, and I owe my life to him. At the age of ten, I wouldhave drowned in the lake at Dunnesford but for his efforts." Vale put back his mask. "I should return to the beauty. Her arms must be sore."

"Even if her constitution is weak," Penelope attempted, "her arse must be a delight. I almost wish I were a man that I might experience the feeling of being inside her."

Her arse should have been delightful, Vale thought as he recalled how easily his cock had slid into the woman due to the immense amount of wetness that had dripped from her cunnie into her sphincter earlier. But there had been something missing with this one – as there had been with all the others. The women were more and more beautiful, yet his drive, his passion, continued to diminish. Perhaps it was only natural once one had experienced all there was to experience, tasted all that a feast could offer.

"Ah, we have some newcomers," Lance noted as a few people who had just walked onto the assembly floor. "Damn me, that brunette looks like Charlotte, but who is the one next to her with the lackluster brown hair and emerald necklace?"

Vale narrowed his eyes at the three emeralds separated by two small diamonds and laced together with silver. At first, he paled. Then his jaw hardened as he answered, "My wife."